The chemise was cut even lower than the dress. As the lady moved toward him and bent over, Morgan had a view of miles of milk-white, nicely curved flesh.

"Mind telling me why you're in my room, Rose?"

"Sure," she said as she rubbed his back. "I like making new friends. I'm good at it." Her washing took on a different twist as her hands, soapy washcloth in her right, trailed down his chest, describing slow circles across his abdomen.

"Look, Rose . . ."

"*Now!*" she suddenly hollered, and leaped back as three men kicked their way through the door. Morgan somersaulted from the tub, coming up wet and naked and savage.

Grabbing Rose's arm he spun her and then sent her flying into the men behind her. A gun thundered in the close confines of the room and Shelter didn't stay around to play anymore.

He leaped out the open window . . .

LAY OF THE LAND #28

BY
PAUL
LEDD

ZEBRA BOOKS
KENSINGTON PUBLISHING CORP.

ZEBRA BOOKS

are published by

Kensington Publishing Corp.
475 Park Avenue South
New York, NY 10016

First printing: August 1987

Printed in the United States of America

1.

Boz Hawkins rolled over in bed and gave the old lady the elbow again. Damn that snoring. He yawned, looked out the window, and then leapt from his bed, hitting the floor just as the shotgun blast ripped the window of his cabin into flying shards of glass and splinters of wood, shredding the curtains hanging there.

Boz screamed with pain. He tried to get to his feet and make for his rifle, but he couldn't do it. His leg was half blown off, the bone shattered badly. The old woman was shrieking hysterically and that was worse than the damn snoring—couldn't she do anything quiet!

Boz dragged himself across the floor. His rifle, a .50 caliber Sharp's repeater, leaned against the wall beside his bureau. The old lady shrieked again and Boz turned back angrily to shout at her, but he never got a chance. The front door was battered down, the heavy plank-and-iron-strap contraption falling to the floor as the three gunmen burst through, their weapons stabbing flames, sending lead into every corner of the room.

The old lady quit shrieking. Her head was half blown off by a Winchester bullet. Boz himself was looking up into the twin muzzles of a scattergun. He put a hand out defensively and had it blown off as buckshot riddled his chest and sent him flopping back to the floor to lie in a dark smear of his own blood.

"Torch it," one of the gunmen said.

"What about scalping 'em?"

"Oh, yeah, okay. Drag Hawkins outside and take care of that. Then torch this place. We don't want to hang around."

In five minutes the Dakota cabin was a torch spewing leaping flames and smoke into the star-filled sky, the gunmen already long gone, vanishing back onto the plains.

The tall man with the cold blue eyes swung down from his paint pony in front of the headquarters building at Fort Randall on the Missouri River just above the Niobrara junction. He stood dusting himself off for a time, squinting into the sunlight and dust as he looked around the fort.

He wore a faded blue shirt and buckskin pants. Around his lean hips was a gunbelt with a low-riding stag-handled Colt revolver and a big leather-handled bowie which rode behind. In the scabbard of his saddle was a well-used Winchester repeater, caliber .44–40.

The tall man tugged his battered, fawn-colored hat on again and strode past two approaching cavalry soldiers to enter the building.

"Who the hell's that?" one of the soldiers, a redhead, asked.

"The new scout, looks like," the other one answered.

The tall man closed the door behind him and stood staring at a heavy-jowled sergeant with rolled-up sleeves and watery brown eyes.

"Help you?" the NCO asked, barely stifling a yawn.

"My name's Morgan. I'm here to see the captain."

"You the new scout?"

"That's right."

"I'm Bill Stoner. First Sergeant. You got any problems, you bring 'em to me, Morgan," the NCO said, looking Morgan up and down as if he didn't see much there worth measuring.

"All right, Stoner. As a matter of fact, I've got a problem right now."

"Yeah? Such as?"

"Such as I want to see the captain and you won't move your lard ass out of that chair and tell him so."

Stoner's face went red and then deep violet. His fists clenched. In Stoner's little kingdom he was absolute ruler over everyone but the officers—and they could be managed. No down-at-the-heels civilian was going to come in here and talk to him like that.

Stoner would have liked to walk right over to the smart ass and rip his gullet out, but you didn't take on a civilian in the captain's office.

There would be plenty of time later.

With studied slowness the soldier lifted himself from his chair and strode to the captain's door. He knocked twice stuck his head in and said, "Morgan's here, sir."

Then he pushed the door the rest of the way open and stood aside as Morgan walked past him, not bothering to glance at the sergeant.

Inside, a weary-looking man with broad shoulders and a weather-lined, chiseled face sat behind his desk, tunic unbuttoned. He fumbled with the button, rose at the same time, and started to salute. Morgan shook his head almost imperceptibly. The door was still partly open.

"Mind sending your sergeant away," Morgan said in a low voice.

"Stoner . . ."

"Send him away, please, Captain."

"All right, of course." The captain walked to the door. Morgan heard something about "supply" and then the sound of the sergeant's heavy receding footsteps.

"Now, sir," the captain said, "please sit down. A drink, Colonel Morgan?"

"No drink," Morgan said. "No 'Colonel.'"

"All right. Do you mind . . ." He looked toward the bottle on top of his filing cabinet wistfully.

"Help yourself," Morgan said.

The captain poured—a little shakily—and took his glass back to his desk. He looked at the man across his desk, still not quite accepting the idea that the army was letting an officer of field-grade rank run around the country like this. The man looked like a cowboy, scarred and tanned. His eyes had seen a lot—Captain Amos Shirke had been around fighting men most of his life. He knew a warrior when he saw one.

"You have something for me?" Shirke asked eventually and handed over the letter. It read simply, *This will identify Colonel Shelter Morgan.* (signed) *General Adolph Pomfret.*

Shirke handed the letter back. Morgan rose, walked to the fireplace, lit a match and started the corner of the letter on fire and, when it was going good, dropped it into the fireplace, watching until there was nothing but ash left.

Then Morgan, his face still expressionless, sat down and crossed his legs. "Now then, Captain Shirke, let's have it. What's going on in Dakota?"

Shirke turned his glass slowly, studying it for a minute before he answered. "It started about a month ago. A man named Boz Hawkins and his wife were murdered, their cabin burned. Hawkins was left scalped on the ground."

"You suspected Indians."

"At first, naturally. We've a renegade Cheyenne named Panther who gives us a lot of trouble off and on."

Morgan waited for the captain to go on. He needed another drink before he did. Settling into his story, he told Morgan, "I had one of our Delaware Indian scouts go out and look over the area to see if he could get a line on which tribe might have done it, which way they were heading, anything, you know?" Morgan nodded. "The scout was absolutely sure it wasn't an Indian, not unless they were all wearing white-made boots and riding white horses. They were all shod."

"What killed Hawkins and his wife?" Morgan asked. "Arrows, what?"

"No, a shotgun, it seems. That bothered me too. I guess an Indian here and there carries a scattergun, but it's far from their favorite weapon for making war or hunting buffalo."

"Your man couldn't track them?"

"Not far. They hit the Little Trace, a small creek just north of there, and walked their horses in the water. Before the scout picked them up again it had started to rain."

"I see. Still, it doesn't seem like you've got anything here you can't handle. Why send for outside help?"

"Didn't Pomfret tell you?"

"No." Morgan wagged his head. "I got a wire that

9

said, 'Go.' I came."

"I don't suppose he wanted to put it down on paper," Shirke said. "All right . . ." The captain's voice grew more confidential. He leaned over his desk and opened his hand. A brass button fell out and rolled around. "This was found at the murder site. Regulation cavalry."

Morgan picked it up, turned it around, and put it back on the desk. Shirke's fist closed over it immediately and he tucked it away in his desk drawer.

"Are you telling me you think soldiers were involved in the raid?" Shelter Morgan asked.

"I'm telling you I *don't know*," Shirke said in a taut whisper. "I obviously can't use one of my officers to investigate as long as there's the slimmest chance. The local law won't touch it if soldiers are involved."

"Someone from the provost marshal's office could have taken care of this."

"Those people are all well-known, Morgan! Besides, they come in wearing their dress blues, carrying their orders, and dragging a secretary behind them. You think they would get anywhere? That's why I asked the general for help. I understood he had some small group of—special investigators?"

"That'll do for a description," Morgan said. He had never really thought of Pomfret's secret operators, cut-throats, explosives men, safe-crackers, and outright assassins as "special investigators," but that was as good a term as any.

"Of course . . ." the captain sighed painfully, "that wasn't the end of it. If it had been I would have forgotten it as an isolated incident. People are murdered on the frontier. It's easy enough to get away with. An old grudge surfaces, maybe someone needs a horse. Out in a

10

cabin a hundred miles from anyone you never discover what has happened."

"What else happened?"

"A virtual repeat of the first raid on a farm fifty miles up the Little Trace. A family named Collins was wiped out. Same incident exactly—shotgun through the window, some pretty messy and unconvincing attempts to make it look like Indians did it."

"Still *possible* that it was Indians?"

"Anything's possible, I suppose. But if they were Panther's people or another band of renegades, they've got strange ways of doing things for Indians."

"You didn't happen to come up with a cavalry button at the Collins' place, did you?"

"No. What are you thinking?"

"That maybe someone wants the army blamed," Morgan said.

"No," the captain said. "There were no buttons. But there was a witness."

Shelter's interest deepened. He leaned forward, those cold blue eyes growing intent. "Who?"

"An old Mexican-Indian named Pablo Ruiz," Shirke answered. "It seems he was sleeping in the Collins' barn without having been invited. Says he saw part of it. Says the men he saw riding off were wearing cavalry uniforms."

"Where is Ruiz now?"

"Run off. He reported what he saw to the town marshal and then got scared and took off. Probably thought the army would come after him next."

"You didn't tell me—did you have patrols out that way?"

"We've had patrols out every night with Panther

11

lurking around. Three patrols each night."

"Same people?" Shelter asked.

"Two of the patrols had the same officers in command, but, Morgan—it can't be one of my officers. It makes no damned sense."

"It made sense to someone," Morgan said. He lit his single cigar for the day and leaned back again. "You want me to find out who it is."

"Of course."

Shelter nodded, blowing out a stream of blue smoke. "What's the idea? How am I supposed to go about it?"

"That's entirely up to you. I've let it out that I hired a new scout—you. It sounded reasonable. One of our Delaware scouts got kicked in the head by a shavetail mule recently. I'll put you out in the field alone, searching for Panther supposedly. From there on, do what you have to do. I want these killers brought in. They're trying to stir something up, *what* I don't know."

"Anything special out that way? Up along the Little Trace, I mean?" Shell asked.

"Like gold, maybe? I've asked myself that. There's nothing there that I've heard of but marginal dirt for farming. Little water outside of the creek water, thin soil. I haven't heard of a gold strike in this part of the territory for a year."

"All right." Morgan rose. "I guess there's not much more we can do beyond speculate. Where do I stay?"

"The visiting officers' quarters, I suppose. I'll have—"

"No. Where *would* a scout stay, Captain?"

"Enlisted barracks."

"That'll do." Morgan said, putting out his cigar with his thumb and forefinger before tucking it away in his

12

shirt pocket.

"Morgan," the captain said rising, his chair scraping the floor, "I *want* these men."

"And if it turns out they *are* soldiers?"

"I want them *more*. I can hardly stomach a renegade white, but a soldier who's gone bad is worse than any slimy thing crawling across the earth. Get them."

"I'll want to meet your officers."

"Of course," Shirke said, repeating that pained sigh. "I'll introduce you at commander's call in the morning."

"Until then," Morgan said with a nod. His hand was already on the doorknob when Shirke remembered.

"I didn't tell you, did I?"

"What's that, Captain?"

"Those footprints they found out at the Hawkins place—one set had to have been made by a woman."

The sergeant was still away from his desk when Morgan went back out into the cool Dakota sunlight, still digesting what Shirke had told him in parting.

A woman? Just what in hell would a woman be doing with a band of renegades; red, white, army, whatever in hell they were? It made no sense on the surface, but Shelter was inclined to believe it if the Indian tracker said it was so. Still, many men have small feet, even some big men. It wouldn't hurt to have a talk with the Indian and find out what he had seen, but Morgan didn't even have his name.

Shelter walked his horse to the army paddock and unsaddled, rubbing his pinto down. It was a big horse, not an Indian pony, and that usually suprised people—seeing a pinto that big and deep-chested. It surprised the hostler, a slow-moving, gangly private with a Georgia

13

drawl. The man stood leaning on a pitchfork near the fence, picking at his gapped teeth.

"Big one."

Shelter who had heard it before looked around and nodded.

"You the new white scout?"

"That's right."

"Figured you was."

Shelter slipped the pinto's bit and let it go to work on the fresh hay. Then he walked over to the soldier and, propping a foot up on the rail, asked, "Who'll I be workin' with? I hear there's two Delaware scouts."

"One now. Star Dan got himself kicked in the face. He's over at the surgeon's. Alive, but ain't spoke for a week."

"This Walika . . ."

"He's a funny one. Short, hard as leather, you know. Don't speak much English—or says he don't."

"Where's he now?" Morgan asked.

The soldier shrugged. "Around, I expect. All I've seen is horses' heads and horses' asses all week myself."

"How do they work it? Each of 'em assigned a company, or what?"

"The scouts?" The soldier turned his head and spat, delighting himself by trapping a fly in it. After he got over that he told Shelter, "Walika, he's patrol scout. Star Dan, he's the tracker."

"Tracker?" Shelter felt a cold knot begin to develop in his gut.

"Sure, your job, you know. Go out, look around for sign—Panther's, whoever might be around."

Then it was Star Dan who had been at the cabin and seen the tracks. And was now at the surgeon's. And this

14

Pablo Ruiz was gone—run off, they said. Shelter didn't like the sound of it, not a bit.

He placed his saddle on a sawhorse, shouldered his warbag, and with his Winchester in hand walked to the enlisted men's barracks.

And right into more trouble.

2.

Shelter Morgan stepped into the barracks and unslung his bedroll. The door behind him closed—Morgan had just a glimpse of a trooper going out and pulling it shut. Then there were only the two of them in the room.

Shelter and big Bill Stoner.

"Hello, civilian," the big first sergeant said.

"Hello, Stoner."

"We have to have a little talk, come to a little understanding."

"Do we?" Morgan's eyes went colder yet and for a moment Stoner seemed to have his doubts, but he had been the main bull for a long while and he pressed on.

Stoner stood there, arms hanging, fists clenching and unclenching. "Not very professional," Morgan said to him.

"Damn *professional*. I run things here and you've got to understand that. I run things even if I have to do it by force."

"Even if you have to beat up civilians."

"There's a man outside," Stoner said, watching the door. "No one's going to come in here. We can do it my way—if you're a man— or you can run to the captain and

16

get me busted. Which way's it going to be, Morgan."

Shelter looked around casually. "See an empty bunk, Stoner?"

Stoner couldn't take ridicule and he couldn't take being ignored. With a howl of rage he launched himself at Shell, who stepped aside and tripped the big man, who went down hard between the rows of bunks.

Stoner was to his feet quickly, very quickly for a man of his bulk. There was blood trickling from his nostrils. Morgan had tossed his bedroll onto an empty bunk. Now he tossed his hat there as well, still seemingly ignoring the first shirt.

Stoner moved menacingly toward Shelter, his big fists bunched in front of him.

"I don't need this crap," Shelter said finally.

"You need something, civilian. You need your ass whipped good."

Stoner took a wild swing at Shelter and the tall man ducked, Stoner's fist barely glancing off his skull as he went down. When Shell came up from his crouch he came up hard, driving his right hand into Stoner's flabby belly while his left hooked over the top and landed flush on the sergeant's cheekbone, splitting it open to the bone.

Stoner was wild-eyed as he backed away. It wasn't so much that he hated this man, Morgan, but he was getting whipped and Stoner knew that once it had been shown he *could* be whipped there would be a long line of men waiting for a second crack at him. He had ruled this post with an iron hand, becoming almost a secret government outside of the military code.

He came in on Morgan again. The tall man jabbed a straight left into his face and the blood spewed from a damaged nose. Stoner leaped foward and got his massive arms around Morgan, pinning his arms to his side.

It wasn't the best place for the sergeant to be. Morgan banged down with his forehead, catching that nose again as he drove his knee up into the first sergeant's groin.

Stoner staggered backward, stumbling, and Shelter helped him the rest of the way to the floor with a shocking right hand shot that slammed into Stoner's skull flush with the ear. The big man went down hard, Morgan stepping back to let him topple face-first to the barracks floor.

There was a minute's silence before the barracks door opened and a corporal stuck his head in. "Finished, Sarge?"

"He's finished," Morgan answered as he unbuttoned his shirt.

The corporal gawked and came forward two steps, bent forward at the waist, studying the unconscious NCO with disbelief. He carefully sat Stoner up and patted his cheek.

"Get him out of here," Morgan growled.

"All right, sure . . ." He started to pick the sergeant up by his armpits, but the man was too heavy a load for him.

The corporal said, "I don't think I can make it."

"No technique," Shelter said. He stepped over Stoner, grabbed one ankle and dragged him to the door, the sergeant's head bumping against the floor. He tugged the NCO out the door and off the porch to leave him lying in the dust.

Morgan, shirt half-unbuttoned, straightened up and, hands on hips, took a series of slow breaths. The officer charging up on horseback nearly knocked him over.

The bay horse, sweating, turned and side-stepped

18

while the lieutenant yelled excitedly. "What's going on here! Who in hell are you? You assaulted Sergeant Stoner!"

"Yeah," Morgan drawled. "I assaulted the poor man."

"By God, this is a military post and I won't have this behavior. Who the hell did you say you were?" Morgan told him. "Well, scout," the dark-eyed, long-nosed lieutenant told him, "maybe you'd better get your butt off this post."

"Just what I was thinking," Morgan answered, glancing at Stoner, who had rolled to his hands and knees and was shaking his head like a wounded bull buffalo.

"What happened, Morrison?" the officer demanded of the corporal.

"Well, Lieutenant Ball, it ain't clear to me. I wasn't there."

"No one ever sees anything. All right, scout, clear off the post. You won't be wanted here after my report to Captain Shirke. Clear off, you hear me!"

Morgan just stared at the man. Overage for a second lieutenant, he had hard lines around his mouth as if his girdle was pinching him. "I heard you," Shelter said. Without another word he walked back into the barracks, gathered his gear, and went out.

Stoner was gone when he emerged into the sunlight. Shelter just walked to the paddock, picked up the big pinto, and rode out toward the adjoining town of Rosalia. A hotel room was sounding better all the time. Never hang around where you're not wanted.

He paid for a second-floor room, opened the window to let the river breeze work at the stale cigar smell of the place, and stretched out in the bed, hands behind his head.

It stunk. The whole thing stunk.

19

Where did you start with something like this? Raiders of some color, maybe a woman with them. Taking what? Nothing that anyone knew of. A first sergeant who should have been busted a long while back. What was Stoner's problem? Shelter yawned.

"Should never have gotten myself into this," he muttered, but then there hadn't been any choice. Major General Adolph Pomfret got what he wanted most times.

He had found Shelter in a Mexican jail waiting to be shot. It had been self-defense, but it was the gringo against the locals and nobody cared who had started it. There had been no way out until Pomfret offered to pull a few strings.

In exchange for a favor.

Like accepting a commission in the U.S. Army with the rank of colonel and working for Pomfret.

It stunk. Morgan couldn't have had less interest in anything than being in Pomfret's private army, one designed to take care of problems slightly outside the law, out of the United States' jurisdiction.

He had an interest in living, however.

And there was no way Morgan could just ride away from this now that he was in it. Shelter had a dark backtrail, and if they wanted to, someone in the States could hang him just as legally as the Mexicans could have shot him.

He was in the army.

He couldn't sleep in the middle of the day. A half-hour's nap did the job and he rose to stretch out the kinks, rinse off in the washbasin, and change shirts.

He knew the territory but not well enough. Going out of the hotel he crossed the street to the courthouse and climbed two flights of wooden stairs to the recorder's office.

"Yes?" The kid behind the desk wore pince-nez glasses and had his thin hair slicked down with lard or some such.

"Like to look at a map of the Little Trace area, have a copy if you've got one."

"Again?" the man said, shaking his head.

"Pardon me?"

"You're the third person this month that's wanted a map of the region." He rose sharply, holding his razor-thin body erect. "You *may* look at the map, but I do not have another copy. You may *not* take it from this office, do you understand?"

"You ever been a schoolteacher?" Shelter asked.

"What?"

"Never mind . . . These other people that wanted a peek at the map, what did they look like?"

"I'm sure I don't know. I don't pay attention to our visitors. I have more important things to do."

"You didn't see them at all?" Shell was smiling, but it was a crooked smile and he had eased around the desk to stand very close to the clerk who swallowed hard, his Adam's apple bobbing once.

"One was a man. One a woman."

"That's it?"

"That is all I saw."

Shelter shrugged. That was it then. Most men might at least have had an idea of what the woman looked like: old, young, built properly, or dressed nice. The clerk, he figured, didn't have time for women either.

Morgan was led into a back room where wooden filing

21

cabinets lined one wall, a picture of President Grant hung on another, and a four-chair table filled the center of the room. The clerk found a two-by-three leather-bound book and let it fall to the table. "You'll find what you want in here. Let me know when you are finished, please."

The officious little squirt went out and started to close the door. "Mind leaving that open? It's a little stuffy in here."

The clerk sniffed and sauntered off to his desk, sitting behind it to take care of his important work, which seemed to be staring at sheets of paper and placing a small check in the corner of each with his fountain pen.

Shelter found the page he wanted and looked it over, not learning much. No planned roads or railroad lines or anything like that. He watched the clerk from time to time. Precisely at noon the little man popped up from his desk, took a derby hat from the hatrack, and went out.

Morgan ripped the page from the book, closed it, and walked out tucking the folded map away.

He rode west by north out of town. A cold wind was in his face, shifting the long grass of the plains, lifting his horse's mane. The country rolled some, and here and there were oaks with an occasional pine. Ahead he could see low hills with more timber on them. Beyond those he should find Little Trace, but just now he wanted to see something else.

He found the burned-out house behind a huge charred oak in a small valley and rode slowly on down. There wasn't much left of the Hawkins' place.

Swinging down, Shelter took his Winchester from its scabbard and started a slow tour of the area. What he could find that Star Dan hadn't he didn't know. It had rained since, erasing any tracks. He walked to the back door and kicked at it. It fell away from the hinges and collapsed into a pile of scorched firewood. There wasn't much to see in the house. A bureau, tilted lopsidedly, and the posts of a bed were all that was recognizable.

Shell looked out the window, expecting to see brass shotgun casings, but there were none. Maybe the man had only fired twice. Maybe Star Dan had picked them up.

Shelter crossed the room and stepped out the back door.

And found himself looking square into a rifle muzzle. There was a lady behind the gun, a small one with an oversized coat, sleeves rolled up, with red hair poking out from under a torn hat, too-big jeans. She was young and tiny and hardly menacing. The rifle was big, old, and mean-looking. Shelter's hands lifted.

"You hold it right there, mister, or I'll shoot your balls off."

"Trophy hunter, huh?"

The little lady frowned and squinted down the sights at Shell. "That's not funny."

"Neither is having someone point a gun at you—besides, ladies shouldn't talk like that." Shelter shifted his feet slightly.

"Don't you move! Don't start me talking, don't distract me. I know all the tricks."

"Don't look old enough to have practiced them much," Shelter said. He lowered his hands a little, but the lady gestured up with the muzzle of that big old rifle and Shelter's hands went back up. "What's the trouble here, lady?" he asked.

"I knew'd I finally catch one of you prowling around."

"One of who?"

"You know," she snapped.

"I don't think *you* do," he said. "I think you just want to shoot someone."

"Maybe I do," she said, stretching the words out. It wasn't menacing, only funny. Shelter grinned. "And stop that damned grinning at me."

"How long can you hold that rifle up?" Shelter asked. "I'll bet I can hold my hands up longer. Why don't you shoot, or we'll figure out some other way to do this."

"Another trick!"

"How about if I drop my rifle, slip my gunbelt off, and sit on the ground—over there," he said nodding. "Then you can tell me what's going on."

They did it that way, the blue eye squinting down the sights of that Spencer rifle alert as Morgan slowly moved and finally settled onto the fire-blackened grass.

"Okay." She lowered the rifle. "Who are you?"

"Shelter Morgan. Army scout out of Fort Randall."

"Aha! Star Dan—"

"Star Dan's in the hospital. *Aha*, yourself. Who are you, anyway?" Shell asked.

"Boomer. Boomer Kennedy."

"*Boomer?*"

"Don't you make a crack or I'll let you have it, I swear it. I'm starting to believe I might have the wrong man," she admitted.

"Who did you think you had?"

"One of the raiders. You know about them, right? I live with my dad up north of here. We been riding wary, working wary, hardly sleeping. When two of your neighbors get burned out you've got something to think about."

24

"I guess you do. Why would a raider come back here, Boomer?"

"Hell if I know! Hell if I know why they did this in the first place. We just don't see many stray white men wandering around out here. Our neighbors we know. Soldiers got uniforms. Drifters usually mean trouble."

"I see." Thinking of drifters, Morgan asked, "You know a man named Pablo Ruiz?"

"Old Pablo, sure."

"Haven't seen him around, have you?"

Something flickered across the girl's eyes. Too quickly she answered, "No, I ain't seen him."

She looked to the skies, which were beginning to cloud a little. "I got to be getting home, I expect. You better follow along."

"You want me to go home with you?" Shelter asked, rising.

"Stop grinning! No, damn it, I don't want you to go home with me. I took your horse and hid it off in the willows. Follow along and I'll show you where."

"You're quite an Indian, aren't you," Shell commented.

"I told you—I know all the tricks."

Shelter followed along in silence. Those too-big trousers, he noticed, didn't conceal the outlines of a nice little ass. He wondered if the girl ever wore anything more appealing.

"There it is." She stood aside, pointing toward the pinto. Tucking her rifle under her arm, she removed her hat and tossed her head. Coils of long red hair flew out and drifted in the wind. From the neck up she looked suddenly quite feminine.

"Thanks." Shelter walked to the horse, the girl

25

behind him.

As he swung into the leather she asked, "What did you say your name was?"

"Shelter Morgan. Why, you're going to check up on me."

The faintest of smiles curved her lips. "I'm just asking," she said, and then turned and walked away—swaying a little more, Shelter thought, than she had before.

He watched thoughtfully for a minute and then turned his horse away. By the time he had poked around the Collins' ruined ranch it was getting late enough that he should start back toward town. He hadn't found a damn thing at either place—not counting Boomer Kennedy—but then he hadn't really expected to. He just couldn't afford to overlook a thing.

Besides, the ride had given him his first look at the Little Trace country, and he figured to be spending a lot of time up there. Rolling hills with oaks and pines; a few cedars crowded the creek itself. Away from the creek the land grew monotonously flat then began to rise again slightly before you reached town.

He didn't have a single idea what the raiders were up to as yet. He very nearly never had a thought of any kind again. The horse dipped down into a dry wash and the sharp crack of a rifle lifted Morgan's hat from his head.

There was no time for being fancy. He threw himself from the horse's back as a second shot dusted him. Landing, he rolled into the deepest part of the wash—all of two feet deep.

He caught sight of drifting smoke in the trees beyond but he had no target, even if he did he wasn't going to hit it with the Colt. The pinto with Shell's rifle in the scabbard had wandered off fifty feet to stand watching its master play.

The rifle spoke again and Shell buried his head as one bullet whined off a rock near his arm, splintering it, and a second thudded into the bank behind him.

Whoever it was, he was a damn good shot, but as long as Morgan stayed flat he wasn't going to tag him.

Morgan stayed flat.

An hour and then another passed. No more shots had been fired, but Shelter wasn't going to move if he had to spend the night there, cramped and bleary-eyed. If the bastard wanted him, let him come on down.

But he wouldn't do that, not if he had any brains. He wouldn't come in range of the handgun and take the chance on spending the night in the gulley himself, dead.

Eventually Shelter heard the sound of a horse being ridden off and he lifted his eyes to the sunset skies to catch a glimpse of a distant rider moving along the ridge. Morgan gave him another fifteen minutes just in case and then rose, walking stiffly to the pinto.

It was nearly dark, but Morgan wanted to have a look up on the hillside. By backtracking the sniper's horse he found the spot where the ambusher had hunkered down behind a split granite boulder and done his work. Brass casing littered the ground. They told him nothing except that it was a Winchester—and half the people in the territory carried one.

Neither could he make any sense out of the only other evidence. Impressed very clearly in the dark earth Morgan noticed the bootprint immediately. And even by the dusky purple light he identified it for what it was.

A woman's bootprint.

"Hell, Boomer, I thought we were friends."

27

But Boomer had already had her chance and not taken it. Why ride back and try again? How many ladies could there be out in this hard country, though? How many who wanted to potshot strangers?

Shell shook his head and swung onto the pinto again, lining out toward Rosalia. He wasn't getting any closer at all to the raiders—but they seemed to be getting too close to him.

3.

In the morning Shelter rolled out of his Rosalia hotel bed, dressed, and headed back toward Fort Randall. It was still early, the sun just barely above the horizon, shining brightly on the wide Missouri River.

At Randall the troops were already out and forming up. The scent of beef and cornbread drifted from the grubhouse. Morgan rode to the headquarters building and swung down. He spotted the grim-faced Lieutenant Ball striding down the plankwalk before the building and saw the officer flash him a searing glance before he turned into a door. Morgan followed. He wasn't going to miss commander's call on this morning.

Morgan walked in without knocking and saw four officers standing together, drinking coffee. Ball's face was furious as he turned toward Shelter and started that way.

"You! Didn't I order you off this post? What are you doing here?"

"You didn't hire me, can't fire me," Shelter said quietly. "I'm here because the captain invited me. Got any more coffee?"

"Why, damn you—I've made my report to the

29

captain. If you think you'll be here long, you're mistaken. We deal with troublemakers in short order on this post."

The door at the front of the room opened and Captain Shirke entered, looking around as if he had never seen the small conference room before.

"Be seated, gentlemen," he invited, and they walked to their wooden chairs. The captain cleared his throat. This is . . ." Morgan saw the officer's mouth move in the wrong direction, and for a split second he thought he was going to say "Colonel." He caught himself, "Shelter Morgan, our new scout."

Ball blurted out, "Sir, did you read my report on yesterday's incident?"

"Yes, I did," the captain said icily. "I spoke to Stoner about it. Now then, Morgan, this is Lieutenant Ball. Beside you is Hodges. On the other side of him Lieutenant Michaelson. In front of me is Lieutenant Doran."

Shelter nodded and got stiff nods in return. Lieutenant Hodges was older, thickly built. Maybe a man out of the ranks. Michaelson was bland appearing, prematurely balding. Doran was just a kid with closely cropped yellow hair and a face that was pink with shaving when he probably didn't need one.

"Morgan, as you know, is taking Star Dan's place. I don't know if Star Dan will ever be able to scout for us again, Dr. Finney can't tell me. That means Morgan will be on free-scout, looking for renegade sign." Shirke lifted his eyes. "That means Panther."

The captain proceeded to take reports of the previous day's patrols, named Michaelson officer of the day, and

30

assigned Doran and Ball their patrol areas. Morgan half-listened.

He looked around from man to man. How did you tell a traitor if you saw one? Ball, of course, he already disliked—so it was natural to suspect him—but Morgan had been alive long enough to know that you don't condemn a man because you don't care for his looks or his manners.

At the end of the meeting the officers trooped out. Morgan remained behind with the captain, who led him back into his private office.

"No luck, I take it, Colonel Morgan?"

"Not in one day, no," Shell answered.

"Any ideas?"

"Damn few." Shelter dropped into a chair.

"This business with Stoner yesterday . . ."

"Forget that." Shelter waved a hand. "It seems your first dog is a little rough, though."

"I've never had a complaint before. I've reprimanded him."

"All right. I've got a few things I'd like to do before I leave the post—by the way, you know a family named Kennedy?"

"Kennedy, of course. Ty Kennedy and his daughter. Why?"

"Anything strange about them?"

"Something strange about the girl," Shirke said with a grimace. "She's a hellcat. Her mother died young and Ty's been raising her for ten years. Hasn't done a hell of a good job of it, it seems. He's in his fields from sunup to sundown, the girl does pretty much what she wants. What interests you in them, Morgan?"

"Nothing, except they live on the Trace."

"I see. You mentioned there were several things you wanted to do. May I be of help?"

"With one point, yes. Each officer has an orderly, I take it?" Morgan asked.

"Well . . . yes." The captain was thrown off-stride. "Ball and Doran are sharing one right now, however. I had PFC Lasky on that duty, but he was a thief. Besides, he didn't know how to shine boots. Doran was starting to look like hell. The kid didn't know any better so he put up with it."

"Doran hasn't been in long, I take it."

"*Four* weeks," the captain said incredulously. "Lieutenant Hodges has been in twenty-three."

"He was enlisted, I take it."

The captain looked mildly surprised. "Yes, as a matter of fact. Made warrant officer, and finally on my recommendation he was given a commission. Good Indian fighter, is Lieutenant Hodges."

"And good with the men?"

"He understands their problems."

Morgan asked, "How about Ball?"

"Lieutenant Ball is a competent officer," the captain responded and left it at that. "So's Michaelson, but he spent too much time behind a desk as Quartermaster before he came to us. Hodges is breaking him and Doran both in, actually."

"I see, all right."

"Any reason for all of this, Morgan?"

"I just wanted an idea of who they were, what sort of background they had. Now about the orderlies."

"Yes." Shirke looked as if he had forgotten completely. Morgan had the idea the captain was a morning drinker too. "What is it I can do there?"

"It's going to be hard to do discreetly, I suppose, but I'd like you to ask each of them this: 'Have you had to sew a new button on the lieutenant's tunic lately?'"

"Oh . . ." Captain Shirke's eyes went to the desk drawer where the button Star Dan had found at the Hawkins' place lay hidden. "All right. I'll have them brought over and talk to them one by one." Hawkins rose. "I'll caution them not to talk about it, but such a ruckus over such a trivial matter is bound to set their minds spinning."

"Half an hour be enough time?" Shelter asked, putting on his hat.

"It should be, yes. May I ask where you'll be, sir?"

"At the surgeon's, Captain, at the surgeon's."

"I did it again, damn it," Captain Shirke muttered. "Called you 'sir,' didn't I? And 'Colonel' too now that I think about it. Sorry, but it's damned hard after twenty-five years to call a superior officer 'Morgan.'"

"Work on it," Shelter said dryly. "I've still got some living I'd like to do."

For a long minute after Morgan was gone the captain stared at the closed door behind him. Then, steadying himself with a small whiskey, he made arrangements to have the orderlies brought over.

Shelter strode down the plankwalk and crossed to the surgeon's office. Inside, a small white-haired man with his boots propped up on a table sat reading a Philadelphia newspaper. A dead cigar was poked into his mouth at one corner.

"Can you tell me where I can find Dr. Finney."

The man nodded. "I'm Captain Finney."

"Any chance of seeing Star Dan?"

"You can see him—but he won't see you," the army surgeon answered. "He hasn't come out of his coma. Mind if I ask who you are, young man?"

"Shelter Morgan, new scout. Captain Shirke knows I'm here."

The doctor shrugged indifferently and folded his paper, tossing it aside. He rose and led Morgan to a room where a dark man, his head wrapped in bandages, lay beneath white sheets staring at nothing. Morgan looked for a minute at the injured Delaware and then turned away. The doctor closed the door.

"Skull's badly fractured. Sometimes they come out of it. Sometimes it's just as well if they don't. End up like vegetables. I've seen it before." The doctor's face showed a little frustration with the imprecise science of medicine.

"The wound is consistent with a mule kick?" Morgan asked. The doctor's eyes narrowed.

"A mule did it," Finney said. "Couldn't mistake it."

Still the surgeon was hedging and Morgan asked, "What's the matter, Captain Finney?"

The doctor's hand fluttered in an incomplete gesture. "Well, I'll tell you honestly," he said, sitting at his desk again, his feet returning to the same spot. "The witness said he was kicked. Says Star Dan was trying to hold the mule while a soldier shoed him. Grabbed the tail to turn him and got kicked on the side of the head."

"Isn't that what happened?"

"Maybe."

"Look, Doctor, if you know something, I wish you'd tell me."

The surgeon's eyes grew shrewd. "I might if you told me who you really are, *scout.*" Morgan figured he had

34

asked one too many questions then. He didn't want to fence with the doctor. His answer was brief.

"I can't."

"I thought so," the surgeon said, looking the man up and down. "Don't look concerned. I've got a close mouth." He studied Shelter a minute longer before he shook his head. "All right. I'll tell you what I *think* and why."

The surgeon finally lit his cigar and waved out the match. "The wound's entirely consistent with a mule kick. You could almost trace the shoe on Star Dan's skull where it was depressed."

"But?"

"Give me time, son. But," he said, taking a deep puff on his cigar, "there were wounds on the other side of the skull too. I took a stone the size of a walnut out of his head just above the ear. Quite a few smaller stones."

"What did that indicate to you?" Shelter asked.

"To me?" The doctor studied his cigar tip closely for a moment before he answered. "It looked to me like the mule was walked over a man's skull, Morgan."

"You reported that?"

"Pure conjecture," the doctor shrugged.

"Could he have been hit with something else, clubbed down, and then had someone use the mule to make it look like something else?"

The doctor repeated. "Conjecture. Possible—yes."

"You didn't look into it?"

"Do I look like a Pinkerton man? Besides, there was a witness and his story was credible."

"Who was the witness? The man who was shoeing the mule?"

"That's right."

"What's his name?"

"Why, it was Lasky, I believe. PFC Lasky."

Lasky. Shelter turned and started straight back toward the captain's office. The name had come up before.

Stoner, his nose swollen, cheek bandaged, was at his desk as Shelter entered the orderly room. He glared at Morgan but said nothing as Shell walked to the captain's door, knocked, and proceeded in. The captain was alone in his office.

"Well?" Shelter asked.

"It didn't take long," Shirke replied.

"Had any of your officers had a new button sewn on his tunic recently?"

"Oh, yes," Shirke said. "All four of them, it seems."

"Damn it, that's a big help. Did you call Lasky over too?"

"Lasky? No. I told you he wasn't an orderly anymore. His pilfering finally caught up with him."

"But he was an orderly when the Hawkins' house was raided."

The captain's face darkened. "Yes," he answered quietly. "He was. Sorry, Morgan."

"That's all right. Apparently the button's getting us nowhere. I want to talk to Lasky anyway," Morgan said, and he told him why. The captain's face continued to fall. When Morgan was finished he answered slowly.

"PFC Nance Lasky was a thief. I had him up on articles and sentenced him to thirty days in the stockade."

"Let's go on over to the stockade, I really want to talk to this man, Captain."

"That will be difficult, Morgan," the captain answered

36

numbly. "He escaped last week."

Morgan didn't continue the conversation but he turned it every which way on the way back to Rosalia. The captain had a snakepit at the post and didn't seem to know what to do about it. To tell the truth, neither did Morgan. He wasn't a Pinkerton himself.

"Damn Pomfret!" Why did he choose Morgan to drop into this? Fighting he understood, but detective work was a little out of his line.

He tried to organize his thoughts. Maybe it went this way: Star Dan had found more than he reported. Lasky, maybe in on it, killed him. Another accomplice set him free from the stockade. Pablo Ruiz, bumming around, had also seen something. They had scared him off and killed him.

"Or not," Shelter muttered to the horse. "Hell, maybe Star Dan was kicked by a mule and then stepped on. Lasky got caught stealing from an officer's truck and broke out of the stockade. Ruiz just wandered off again."

There was too damn much circumstance and Morgan felt down inside that someone from the fort was involved in the bloody raids along the Little Trace Creek.

"But maybe not," he said with a sigh. Then he laughed at himself, laughed, and the horse's ears twitched in annoyance. Shelter patted the pinto's neck and said, "How do you like my detective work so far?"

No, he wasn't likely to discover much more the way he was going. The key to it all was out on the plains and that was where Shelter was going to have to go. Smack in the raiders' territory—and in Panther's for that matter. He damned Pomfret another time for good luck and rode into Rosalia.

Dinner in Rosalia's single restaurant was all right if

you liked burned steaks and three or four pounds of fried potatoes and coffee. That was all they had and that was the only way it came.

Shelter had gone hungry too many times in his life to complain and he had too much on his mind to notice much. When he left, at least his belly was full.

He stood outside watching sunset flush the sky pink above Rosalia. A wagon followed by a yapping dog rolled up the dusty street and a single cowboy rode the other way. That was Rosalia's version of nightlife. If they had a saloon Morgan didn't know where it was. He wasn't much of a drinker, but a beer would have been fine.

Not having one he did without and walked back to the hotel. He wanted to have another look at the map he had borrowed from the courthouse and then a bath. He didn't figure he'd have the chance for another one for a time.

The desk clerk sent up a zinc tub and three or four kids began filling it with boiling water from the kitchen. Morgan sat on the bed looking at the map, comparing it to what he had seen, glancing up only when a new bucket of water was delivered.

"That's it, mister," the last kid said, and Shelter flipped him half a dollar. Still looking at the map of the Little Trace area he crossed to the door, kicked it shut, and began undressing with one hand.

Shelter tested the water. It was hot enough to boil coffee and he eased in real gently, finally settling in to parboil away the grime clinging to him. On a stool beside the tub one of the kids had put a washcloth and two towels. A new cake of yellow lye soap was beside them.

Morgan got to work peeling off some of his filthy hide. When the tap sounded at the door he barely turned his head, thinking it was one of the kids returning.

It wasn't.

The lady hadn't been a kid for a long time. She was a full-blown voluptuous woman in a dark low-cut dress, carrying a red fan which matched the little red hat tilted on her head.

"Oops," she said, the fan going before her face so that just a glittering pair of dark eyes showed. "Wrong room, I guess."

"You sure?" Morgan asked, smiling.

She looked him up and down, though there wasn't much to see but head and knees. "Maybe not," she said. Then she toed the door shut again.

Morgan watched her as she walked to his bed and sat down, jumping up and down a couple of times like a kid testing the springs.

"You aren't from around here," she said, putting her fan aside to give Shelter a better view of her handsome face. Maybe the nose was arched too much, the painted mouth a little generous, but she was a fine-looking woman.

Shell had forgotten temporarily about his washing.

"You need some help, don't you, honey," the lady said.

"Do I?"

"Sure. You can't wash your back. Oops! Don't want to get my new dress wet."

In a moment she didn't have to worry about that because it lay crumpled on the floor around her ankles. Wearing bloomers and a chemise she stepped from it.

The chemise was cut even lower than the dress. The tips of her nipples were all that it covered as the lady moved toward him and bent over, giving Morgan a view of miles of milk-white, nicely curved breasts.

39

"Let me have that washcloth, honey, I'm Rose, everybody knows me in Rosalia."

"They do, do they?" Morgan asked as the lady started washing his back from the front so that her breasts were nearly in his face. Morgan's mind was beginning to drift. There was a not-so-slow swelling and lengthening beginning between his legs. "Mind telling me why you're in my room, Rose?"

"Oh, I was waiting for a friend. He never showed up. But I like making new friends."

"You do, do you?" Morgan asked. His shaft was fully erect now, the head of it bobbing on the bathwater's surface.

"Sure," Rose kept rubbing his back. "I like making friends. I'm good at it." Her washing took on a different twist as her hands, soapy washcloth in her right, trailed down his chest, describing slow circles across his abdomen. "Oh look," she said as if she had just found a fuzzy kitten. Her right hand dropped the rag and wrapped itself gently around Shelter's erection.

"Look, Rose . . ."

"Now!" she suddenly hollered, and she leaped back as three men kicked their way through the door. Morgan somersaulted from the tub, coming up wet and naked and savage.

He scooped up the stool beside the tub and smashed it into the face of the first thug. Rose screamed and he glanced at her. Grabbing her arm he spun her and then, kicking her in her ass, he sent her flying into the two men behind her. A gun thundered in the close confines of the room and Shelter didn't stay around to play anymore.

He leaped out of the open window and hit the roof rolling. A second shot was fired, tearing up the shingles beside Morgan as he kept going, dropping to the street below.

He ducked under the eaves and pressed himself against the wall, teeth chattering, eyes moving up and down the street. He heard footfalls in the room above and then there was only silence. Morgan looked down at his hand and was surprised to see the towel there.

It was useful enough. He wrapped it around his hips and strolled into the lobby of the hotel. Marching up to the desk clerk he said, "Sorry, that room isn't satisfactory."

4.

Morgan, freshly stocked up with cartridges and provisions, rode out onto the long plains in the morning.

He hadn't been real smart about things the night before, he realized, but when a woman starts taking off her clothes, offering to help you with your bath, even the best men lose a little edge off their smarts.

Thinking about it, that Rose hadn't been such a bad-looking woman at all. Under other circumstances . . . For some reason he found himself thinking about Boomer Kennedy, the way her little ass wiggled as she walked, that spark in her eyes and mountain of untamed red hair.

And that big rifle.

Morgan would have given a dollar or two to know where Boomer was when the sniper was taking potshots at him.

Morgan's thoughts broke off. The country was fairly flat, much of it dry grassland, with sage and greasewood growing here and there in clumps. It was one of these clumps of brush that caught his eye now.

Not the brush itself, but something behind it. Something that didn't belong among the dry browns and washed-out grays of the land. Something bright yellow.

Morgan turned the pinto that way, easing his rifle out of his scabbard. The way things had been going he wasn't exactly in a trusting mood.

In the brush was a man, but Morgan didn't need his rifle. He was as dead as you can get, sprawled out across the ground, one arm bent under his back.

The yellow was the yellow of a cavalry scarf. The blue was the blue of the soldier's uniform. Morgan swung down, his eyes searching the country around him, noting without conscious thought the thunderheads building over the hills beyond.

Shell grimaced as he crouched down to look the soldier over. His scalp had been taken, his eyes carved out. Shelter patted the man down and found a wallet in his hip pocket. Squatting back on his heels he rummaged through it, but he already knew.

There was a letter inside with the man's name on it, an old letter from San Antonio in which some passionate young lady told the soldier how much she appreciated his anatomy.

PFC Lasky must have appreciated it to carry the letter so long and so far.

Morgan dropped the wallet and stood, looking down at the former orderly, petty thief, jail-breaker. "They busted you out, didn't they pal?" Morgan muttered.

Busted him out and then silenced him for good.

Shelter started slowly circling the area, looking for tracks. Lasky hadn't been dead long, maybe a night and a day, and there should be some sign remaining.

There was, but that too brought a frown to Morgan's face. Three horses had been in the area—one of them, presumably Lasky's, was shod. The other two were Indian ponies. And, clearly marked out in the earth where the horsemen had mounted, were the signs of moccasins.

Maybe Lasky had just run into some bad luck. It could be he had stumbled into a couple of Panther's warriors and paid for it. Shelter still didn't like it. In the back of his mind he had doubts about so simple an explanation.

Swinging aboard the big pinto he started north, riding toward where the Kennedy place should be located. If Panther was in the area, the settlers should be warned. At least, he told himself that was his reason for riding that way.

It was a good enough reason, but unnecessary as it turned out. Riding along the creek until he found the small log buildings scattered among the oaks, he saw the cavalry soldiers in the yard of the Kennedy house.

They stood in groups of two and three beside their horses, looking toward Morgan as he rode up. He recognized none of them, but one man knew him by name.

"Hello, Morgan. How's things out there?"

"Saw some Indian sign." Shelter swung down and wiped his forehead with his cuff. "Two strays, looked like. Might have been scouting ahead. Any reports of Panther?"

"Not that I heard."

"Who's your officer?" Shelter asked.

"Lieutenant Ball." The soldier nodded. "He's in the house talking to Kennedy."

It would be Ball, Shelter thought. He couldn't just get on his horse and ride out, so he went to the cabin door, rapped, and was answered by a hoarse voice inviting him in.

Shelter swung the heavy plank door in and stepped

44

into a tiny, neat cabin. Ball stood near the stone fireplace, drinking coffee, one elbow on the mantel. His dark eyes narrowed as Shelter strode in.

The man with the chin whiskers had to be Ty Kennedy. There was no sign of Boomer, though there was a second room, curtained off with an Indian blanket beyond.

"Kennedy, Morgan," Ball managed to say. The old man had more manners. He stood and offered Shelter a work-hardened gnarled hand.

"Glad to meet you."

"Morgan's our new roving scout," Ball explained.

"I came by, Mr. Kennedy, to let you know that there are at least a couple of Indians in the area. Found their sign and a man scalped." Shelter glanced at Ball to see how the officer took this news. He didn't look surprised or shocked. "A soldier."

"You know who it was?" Ball asked.

"Lasky."

Ball shrugged, "Small loss. He would've been shot for desertion anyway."

Even Ty Kennedy was surprised at the callousness of the officer's remark. True, Lasky was no loss to anyone, but he had been one of Ball's soldiers.

The door banged open and a redheaded whirlwind swept in. Hatless, the diminutive woman took three steps and then halted, looking at the men's faces.

"What's going on around here?" Boomer demanded.

"There are renegades around," her father told her. "You stick closer to the house for a while."

Ball said, "If I were you, I'd give some thought to pulling out until this is settled down out here, Mr. Kennedy. Go into Rosalia. No sense in taking chances with your life or your daughter's."

45

"If I don't stick I lose the place," Kennedy said, "and I don't feel like starting over. I'm too old for it. If I don't bring these crops in, Lieutenant, I'm done."

"Your daughter . . ."

"If Dad sticks, I'm sticking," Boomer said, and that was that. Even her father didn't try to argue with her. Maybe he hadn't had much success with that over the years.

"Well, stay closer to home," Ty Kennedy said quietly.

Boomer just nodded. She was looking hard at Shelter Morgan in a way that wasn't easily defined. Partly hostile, it was more than that.

"So he *is* an army scout," the girl said.

"Supposedly," Ball answered with a self-amused smile.

"He's the one I told you about, Dad. The one I saw prowling around the Hawkins' place. I didn't believe the son of a bitch."

"Boomer," her father said, wincing at her choice of words.

"Sorry, Dad. I don't think I shocked either of these two."

"What were you doing at the Hawkins' place?" Ball asked, his smile sliding away from his mouth.

"My job. Having a look around. Star Dan can't tell us much more, can he?"

"He reported everything he saw to the captain. I saw the report."

I'll bet you did, Shelter thought but didn't say. "He might have missed something—anyone can."

"Not Star Dan," Ball argued.

And maybe that was why he was at the surgeon's right now.

"If you boys wait a while," Ty Kennedy said, "my daughter will boil up enough coffee for all your men." Boomer didn't look thrilled with the idea.

"No thanks," Ball answered, taking his hat from the table. "We're going to proceed up Little Trace. I'm three hours behind right now. I just wanted to stop by and see how you were, let you know the army's out this way."

"That didn't keep the Collins' or the Hawkins' place from being hit," Boomer snapped.

Ball just stared at her. "Good-bye now, Kennedy. Morgan, you're riding with us."

"The captain wants me on free scout," Shelter said.

"Circumstances have changed. I'll explain to the captain. I'm giving you an order," Ball said, glancing at the civilians to see if they were properly impressed. "You're not going to disobey a direct order, are you, Morgan?"

"No." No damn it, he couldn't. A slight flaw in the plan he and Pomfret had laid out. There was no way a supposed army scout was going to flat-out disobey an officer's order. Morgan was trapped. For the time being his snooping was on hold.

Was Ball doing this on purpose, to get Shelter out of the area, or did he really want a scout? Maybe he was just being obnoxious—that was in character for him.

Shelter followed Ball outside. He couldn't help noticing that Boomer's eyes tracked him all the way.

"I don't owe you an explanation," Ball said as he mounted his bay horse, "but I'll give you one. We're still short a scout. Walika is out with Doran—the captain figures the kid needs all the help he can get. If what you say about the renegades being in the area is true, I want to find them and if possible engage them. I need a scout to

47

find the Indians. *All right?*" he asked with sarcasm.

"Yes, sir," Shelter answered. "If you need me, I'll go along."

Ball nodded smugly. He had demonstrated his authority to his own satisfaction. The soldier Shelter had talked to earlier said, "Don't mind him, Morgan. He's always that way."

"Makes it kind of hard, doesn't it?"

The pock-faced corporal shrugged. "It all pays the same. I'd rather be in Hodge's company, for sure. Sometimes old Harry Hodges even forgets he's an officer now. But it *could* be worse than riding with Ball."

Shelter ducked his head as they rode under a massive, gnarled oak limb. "You mean Doran?"

"That's right. How'd you like to be riding under a man who's been in the army *four weeks?* Michaelson is some better, but he's more a rules-and-regulation man than a combat officer. Can't take a quartermaster and throw him out in the field either. He don't much know what he's doing." The corporal nodded to the head of the column. "Ball knows what's going on out here. He's at least a warrior."

Morgan looked at the narrow back of the hooked-nosed, abrasive lieutenant ahead of them and wondered just what kind of warrior he was.

"Morgan! Forward!" the officer yelled just then, and with a nod to his companion, Shelter heeled the paint pony forward to ride beside the lieutenant.

"Bluffs are starting to rise," Ball said, looking upward. "I don't want to be caught in the riverbottom if Panther is around. Get yourself up one side or the other and have a look around."

"Yes, sir."

48

"If you don't catch up with us before then, we're camping at Owl Hollow—you know where that is, by any chance?"

"I have a map," Morgan said, and the lieutenant gave him an odd look as he turned the pinto away from the column and started looking for a way up the north slope out of the canyon.

The bluffs were around seventy feet high, and it wasn't any easy climb, but with much dust and a lot of rolling rocks sent into the canyon below, the pinto finally managed to pull itself up and over and onto a grassy flat.

Shelter swung down to give the horse a breather and watched Ball and his men wind their way up the Little Trace. Shell crouched, holding the horse's reins. He was glad to be away from Ball, but that didn't set him free to do the work he had been sent to do. If there were renegade Cheyenne around, Morgan couldn't let them hit the soldiers without warning.

He smiled to himself, pulled out his cold cigar, and lit it, cupping his hands around the match. No matter what he did, he didn't seem to be able to get out of the army. He had done five years in the C.S.A., coming out a captain. Then Pomfret had taken over his life, saving Shelter's neck for a price. Now there was Ball's private little war.

The wind blew the ash from Shelter's cigar and he looked around to see that the thunderheads were still building. The wind was colder, much stronger up here. It was going to rain, damn it all. That was no good for tracking of any sort.

The horse rested, Shelter wound his way across the flat, working through the trees—pinyon pine and cedar. He studied the ground as he followed the game trail, looking for Indian sign, but his eyes constantly lifted to

49

the horizon as well, searching for smoke, or color.

The land was more broken here, ridges of granite with pines, wind-bent and gnarled, clinging tenaciously to them. From time to time Shell rode to the edge of the bluff to keep an eye on the patrol and to look toward the far side of the canyon.

He saw no one, discovered no tracks for the first two hours. When he did come across something, it wasn't what he had expected.

There was a spot along the ridge where earth had been freshly crumbled away—living roots still projected from the ground. Drifting that way Morgan slowed his horse and then dismounted, walking forward. There were horsetracks there, and farther on the bootprints of two white men. One of them had smoked a cigarette while they waited and watched. Watched for what? The cavalry? Sure, if they were with the raiders. They wouldn't want to tangle with an army patrol.

The men had ridden off in quite a hurry, to the north. If they knew where the soldiers were, the raiders now knew where they *weren't* as well.

And where there were no soldiers they could raid with impunity.

Morgan hesitated. There was no hope of riding to Ball, reporting, and getting back before dark. It probably wouldn't have done any good to let Ball know what was happening anyway.

Maybe he already knew.

Shelter started tracking north. Maybe the two men whose tracks he'd spotted had nothing to do with the raiders, but if that was so it was a long coincidence that they had been crouched there, watching the army patrol pass through the gorge.

50

Morgan lifted his eyes to the sky. There was no longer any doubt that it was going to rain, it was just a matter of when. A sheet of gray had been draped across the sky and the wind, already brisk, was beginning to howl through the trees.

He untied his slicker as he rode and shouldered into it.

When it began to storm it came down harder than he had expected. A wash of rain slanted down violently from lightning-filled skies, almost erasing the landscape ahead. Within minutes the tracks were invisible and Shelter cursed his bad luck. He was stuck between and betwixt now—far from Owl Hollow and Lieutenant Ball, with no hope of tracking the watchers.

Lightning struck near at hand, filling the air with sulfurous stench. The following thunder rattled Shell's eardrums and caused the usually steady pinto horse to balk briefly. The trail ahead was suddenly black and sodden, lost among the trees.

There was nothing to do but look for a place to hole up. Night was coming in and the thunder promised more storming.

He kept the horse plodding onward, hoping that he didn't ride straight into an outlaw camp in the darkness the weather had brought. There wasn't much in the way of cover available, though all Shell wanted was a bluff, a stand of boulders, something to break the wind and maybe cut the rain a little.

And then there was.

He hadn't been riding in luck, but suddenly he spotted a form that didn't belong in nature and he swung the pony that way. The squat, dilapidated cabin emerged from the darkness to take on form and substance.

51

"Everything can't go wrong, I guess," Morgan said under his breath.

He halted the pinto, looped his reins around a low pine limb, and unholstered his Colt. There was no smoke rising from the ancient cabin's chimney and no sight of light or any livestock. Still, he wasn't in the frame of mind to take any chances.

He circled to the back of the cabin, and with his back to the unbarked logs that made up the wall of the place eased toward a back window which was just large enough to peer into—or shoot out of.

Morgan had his look although there was little enough to see. A flash of white lightning revealed a dead, musty, cobwebbed, dirty ramshackle interior.

It couldn't have looked better to a man lost and soaked through, cold and weary.

He unsaddled the pinto and left it where it stood. Returning to the cabin with his bedroll and warbag, he kicked the door in and entered the deserted house.

The roof was leaking in half a dozen places, but it was leaking a hell of a lot more from the sky outside. It would do. Half-feeling his way around in the near darkness, Shelter found the ancient bed, its mattress long gone, the leather strapping that had supported it still strong enough to hold his weight. He laid his bedroll out on it and moved around the cabin looking for critters before returning to the door briefly to watch the cold rain slant down through the pines.

There was someone out there. Morgan could see a dark stain on the curtain of rain and then the vaguest outline of horse and rider. He didn't relish being caught inside the cabin in case of a fight. He needed freedom to move around.

Snatching up his Winchester he slipped out the door and made for the trees. He was there watching when the lone rider—the cabin's owner?—dismounted behind the house and went on in.

Shell looked around to make sure there wasn't someone else following then moved back to the door.

"Hold it right there," he said, levering a shell into the rifle's chamber, sighting on the middle of the intruder's back.

"Trophy hunting?" the lady asked and she slowly turned toward Shelter.

"Boomer!"

"Starting to really come down out there," she said, removing her hat, snapping the water from it so that her fire-red hair spilled out. "See you found Old Man Cooney's cabin."

"Who's Cooney?" Shelter asked lowering the rifle as he stepped in and closed the door, cutting out the howling wind.

"Don't worry about him. He's long gone. Dead. He was chopping wood, missed, and got his leg. By the time he made it to our place he was already a goner."

Boomer seemed to know where everything was. She moved to a small pantry, took out a candle and lit it. The dull glow of the wick illuminated the dusty interior softly.

"I thought you were with the army," Boomer Kennedy said, sitting on a wooden chair, clasping her hands between her knees.

"I got lost."

"I believe it!" she laughed. "Shelter, when you go out in the rain, you really ought to wear a slicker or something," Boomer said.

Morgan looked down at his rain-soaked clothing. "I had one on. Someone comes slipping up on you, you don't take time to dress."

"I scared you?"

"Just being wary. What are you doing here, anyway?"

"Looking for you. I have something to tell you. Say—you really ought to get out of those clothes. We can't have a fire, I don't expect?" she asked, looking toward the squat stone fireplace.

"No. It might bring company."

"Well?" She shrugged. "Go ahead and strip down. I won't look."

The candlelight on her face revealed a slight smile. Shelter shrugged. He had never been particularly shy, and he didn't relish sleeping in wet clothes. He shucked his shirt and trousers, slipping his blanket over his shoulders. It was cold anyway, damn cold. Boomer was shaking with it.

"No riding tonight," she said.

"No, you got a bedroll?"

"I didn't plan on being out this long. When the rain started I made for the cabin." She was still trembling.

"Maybe you'd better get out of your things too."

"You'll look," she said impishly.

"Not if you don't want me to."

"Hell—lay down on your bunk. Look at the wall."

"You got all kinds of rules, lady."

"You want to be responsible for me catching pneumonia? Do what I told you, tall man."

Morgan looked at her for a long moment, shook his head, and then climbed into his bunk, face to the wall. He heard small rustling noises and a natural curiosity came over him. Rolling his head slightly he opened one eye a little.

Damned nice.

She had a compact, bouncy little body with full round breasts, very firm with rosebud nipples. Her ass was full and firm, the triangular patch of reddish hair where her smooth white thighs joined interesting.

"Damn it all," Boomer said, "You're peeking."

"Yeah, I'm peeking," Shelter said, watching as she folded her trousers and draped them over the chair.

Boomer stepped to the candle and blew it out. "There, you lousy Peeping Tom." She was silent for a minute. "Now what do I do? You have a spare blanket?"

"No," Shelter said. "No spare. Come on, Boomer," he said, lifting the edge of the blanket. "I'll keep you warm."

The floorboard squeaked slightly and then she was in beside him, her flesh cool, her ass thrust out against Shell. "No tricks," she muttered as he put his arm around her. "Just keep me warm."

"Sure, Boomer. I'll just keep you warm."

She rolled toward him suddenly, her hair brushing his face. "Can I touch them?" she asked out of the darkness.

"Touch what?"

"You know. My trophy. Your balls." Her voice was whispery now.

"Just touch them?" Shelter asked, nuzzling her ear.

"Sure. I seen men before, but I never— I just wanted to feel them once," she said.

"I don't know," Morgan said. "No tricks?"

"No tricks," she agreed and Morgan felt her small hand drift down between his legs, cup his sack. It was a nice way to help warm him, he decided.

"Well?" he asked.

55

"Trophy size," she said.

"Find anything else you like?" Morgan asked her as his hand slid down her spine to roam her splendid, tight little ass.

"I don't know." Her hand moved around tentatively and found Shelter's shaft. She gave a little gasp of surprise and held it tighter, moving nearer yet to him. "I'll just hold that a while, all right?"

"It's all right," Morgan said, kissing her ear again, feeling her shudder.

"But that's all I'm doing, right? No tricks?"

"No tricks," Morgan agreed.

They lay there for a long minute, Boomer's body rigid, her fingers moving lightly against his erection. Morgan didn't move. The woman sat up abruptly, the blanket falling away from her shoulders.

"Damn it all, Shelter. When I say no tricks, I don't always mean no tricks! I'm a lady, damn you, I can't say I want you to fuck me!"

"What do you want?" he asked, tugging her down by the nape of her neck to find her parted lips with a deep kiss. She whispered her answer.

"I want you to fuck me."

"But no tricks."

"No tricks."

5.

There was no trick to it at all. Within minutes Boomer was riding high, straddling Shelter, his shaft buried deep in her moist warm flesh as she thrashed about, wriggling from side to side, driving herself down against his swollen flesh as Morgan's hands roamed her breasts, teasing her nipples, gripping those firm little globes tightly.

Boomer threw her head back and her hands covered Shelter's. She squeezed her own breasts hard and pounded at him with her pelvis, making small birdlike noises deep in her throat, gasping for breath as she rose to a hard climax which shook her body like an earth tremor and made her inner body collapse into wetness.

Leaning forward she pressed against Shell, biting his neck, shoulders, ears, clawing at him as he humped against her, his back arching as he filled her with his own sudden climax.

She lay still, puffing, her fingers clenching and unclenching, her heart pounding as her hands roamed Shelter's hard body. Shell tugged the blanket up over her bare back and shoulders.

"Warmed up now?" he asked.

"Good and warm."

"Boomer, what brought you after me?" he asked. "You said you wanted to tell me something. You never got around to telling me what it was."

"I got sidetracked," she whispered. Her finger ran around Shell's ear as she spoke.

The rain fell against the sod roof of the cabin, making a pleasant sound. Boomer's body was warm against Shelter's; the world was completely dark except for the intermittent flashes of lightning. Finally she told him.

"You asked about Pablo Ruiz. You said you wanted to find him."

"No," Shelter said. "I never said I wanted to find him."

"But you do, or you wouldn't have asked about him."

"Where is he?" Shelter asked.

Boomer was slow in answering. "He's an old man, Shelter, and he's pretty scared. It's not too easy for a man like him around here. He's half Indian, half Mexican. We haven't got six Mexicans around for five hundred miles. To everyone else he's just a half-breed."

"I understand," Morgan said.

"I hope so. One time there was trouble in Rosalia. A girl was abused near the schoolhouse. They took Pablo in even though he was five miles away and working at the time. They would've hung him, I think, except the real culprit turned himself in out of guilty feelings."

"I see."

"Pablo—" she sat up, pushing at her hair as Shell's hands found their way to those lovely breasts again, "Pablo stays away from town, stays away from people. I'm probably his only friend."

"How did you get to know him?"

"He used to come around the ranch. When I was little

he showed me how to make toys, carve whistles and tops and things like that. He's eaten with us, slept on our floor."

Shelter was thinking. It must have taken a lot of courage for Ruiz to report what he had seen of the raiders to the town marshal after nearly being railroaded once before. It was no wonder, however, that the man didn't care to be found.

"You know where he is," Shelter prompted. Boomer had fallen silent, enjoying the caress of Morgan's strong hands.

"I know. I told him about you."

"About me? What did you tell him?"

"That you were special. That you were some sort of government undercover man."

Morgan's hands stopped moving. "What makes you think a thing like that, Boomer Kennedy?"

"Caught you, didn't I?" she laughed. "Your hand just stopped. Your body went rigid. I wish I'd have seen your face."

"You get funny ideas, lady."

"Do I? I'm not stupid. I saw you out looking around the Hawkins' place. No sense in a scout doing that again. There couldn't have been any tracks left. Second thing is, the army might bring in a white scout, even though they haven't had one at Fort Randall for all the years it's been there, but it doesn't seem they'd bring in someone who doesn't even know the territory."

She was silent, waiting for Shelter to admit something perhaps, but he wasn't about to. He only wondered who else had such powers of reasoning in the area. Like Ball, who could add that to what he already knew, like the odd protection Captain Shirke had given him after the brawl with Stoner.

"Where is Ruiz?" Shelter asked.

"Up in the hills farther. I said I'd take you out there in the morning to talk to him. He's scared but he wants someone to know the whole story."

"I want to hear it, Boomer, but I can't go. Not tomorrow. Lieutenant Ball is expecting me back."

"What's more important?" she asked.

"It's not that. It's just that I *have* to report back. I'm supposed to be out looking for Panther and his renegades."

"But Pablo may get nervous if we don't show up. He may pull up stakes and we won't see him ever again."

"Won't he talk to you?"

"Pablo is *very* Mexican," she answered. "You don't talk business with women where he comes from and you don't scare them with horror tales. They sit by the fire and wonder what the men are doing."

"I see. The best I can do is check back in with Ball in the morning, make an excuse to ride back out and meet you. How far away is Ruiz?"

"Not far. Ten miles maybe."

"That might work, then. There's another thing, Boomer—you didn't happen to see two white men riding out this way earlier in the day, did you?"

"On the bluff?"

"Yes."

"The soldiers, you mean," she said.

Soldiers. "You sure, Boomer? It's important."

"If they're the ones you mean. Sure, while I was looking for you they went past me, maybe a quarter of a mile off, riding north like they were in a stakes race. They

60

were soldiers for sure, Shelter."

Morgan tugged the woman back down and clung to her for warmth in the night. Soon she was sleeping, but Shell stayed awake a long time afterward, trying to puzzle out the mad game. Nothing fit, not a damn thing, and after a time he too slept while the rain fell down.

Boomer was gone when he woke up, surprisingly. Morgan had survived a long while in wild country and he wouldn't have believed anyone could slip away from next to him, dress, and leave without awaking him, but the girl had done it.

Morgan's stomach was growling but he didn't want to take the time to dig out the dry biscuits and jerky from his pack or make coffee—it wasn't worth it; besides he still wasn't sure he wanted smoke rising from this cabin.

Outside it was cloudy, but through a gap in the clouds early sunlight shafted down in a red-gold column. The pines were heavy with water, the ground sodden. The pinto looked at him with accusing eyes as he approached with the saddle and blanket.

The Indian came from out of the tree, war hatchet raised overhead, and Shelter hurled the saddle at him, falling to the ground on his back as he did.

The saddle hit the Indian and knocked him back a step. Morgan took that split second of time to draw the big blue Colt and fire twice into the chest of the renegade.

Shelter saw the man buckle up and plow face first into the ground, but he saw that only out of the corner of his eye. He was already moving. It was a good thing he was.

Ducking low and dashing toward the shelter of the pines as the pinto reared up in terror, Morgan drew a spate of gunfire. A bullet ripped into the bark of a massive pine, tearing out a chunk of wood the size of Morgan's fist, showering him with bark as he dove to the ground and rolled aside.

Shelter thumbed two fresh cartridges into his pistol as he knelt there, waiting for a target. The renegades were silent in the woods, making no more sound than the wind in the pines.

Boomer—had she gotten away or had the bastards caught her?

The hint of a sound to Morgan's left brought his Colt around and he tracked onto the charging Indian. A single shot from the muzzle of the Colt ripped through the Indian's skull and jerked him back as a bullet from the attacking renegade's rifle whipped past Morgan's ear and buried itself in the dark earth.

Morgan was up and moving. That was two down. How many were there? He thought he had seen three altogether, but things had happened very fast; besides, there could have been others trailing these, others who would come on the run at the sound of shots. The thing to do was get out of there, but the pinto was across the clearing now and to cross it Shelter would have to put his life on the line.

He stayed put.

Easing to his belly he elbowed and kneed his way forward through a dense tangle of vines to lie still, watching, the Colt wrapped tightly in his hand.

He could just see the cabin beyond the clearing. His saddle and blanket were still there, near the house, but the pinto had run off—or been led off.

Shelter shivered and switched the grip on his gun. It could be a long wait, but the cold and the waiting beat

62

the grave.

He never saw the last one. The rifle report behind Morgan turned him and his gun came up, but already the renegade was toppling forward, blood leaking from his mouth and nostrils as he pressed a hand to the gaping exit wound in his guts.

The pint-sized woman emerged from the woods then and Boomer, hand on her hip, stood looking down at Morgan. "Better get going," she said.

"I thought you were long gone."

"I was going, but I saw these three heading this way. I pulled off the trail and followed them back."

Morgan looked at the dead renegade and then with new admiration at Boomer. "You could be a kind of handy girl to have around."

"I can do everything. What I can't do, I'm willing to learn."

Morgan had rarely seen a woman with nerves like this. She had just killed a man, blown away his spine, and she could stand there and smile. He asked her about it.

"Shit, Shelter. I've lived out here for most of my life. We've had renegades crawl in our windows, had 'em try to burn the house down. We've had white no-goods try to kill Dad, rape me, you name it. I learned how to shoot early and I learned right. I either fight when I have to out here or lock myself up in the house and sit looking fearfully at the windows. You see which way I chose. I got your pinto, by the way. You really ought to keep better track of that animal, Shelter, seems like you're always losing it."

Shell retrieved his saddle and blanket while Boomer brought the pinto around. "Your dad'll be missing you,"

Shelter said, cinching up his saddle.

"Yes, he will. But he gave up worrying about me. Said he'd live longer that way. I'm gone a day or two, three sometimes, and he don't say much."

"I'll wager Lieutenant Ball has something to say," was the last comment Morgan made before he gave Boomer a light kiss and sent her on her way. He was right: When he finally caught up with the patrol, Ball had a lot to say.

"Where in *hell* have you been, Morgan! Out for a Sunday ride?"

"Trying to do my job, sir."

"Your job! You didn't even show up at Owl Hollow last night. We've been riding three hours this morning and finally you put in an appearance. Look, Morgan, you follow my orders or you're through with the army."

"That's a thought," Morgan said under his breath. He tried to explain, briefly, about having spotted tracks on the bluff, getting caught out in the rain, and finally being hit by renegades this morning.

Ball wasn't buying it. "You had no business wandering off after renegades. I wanted you on that bluff watching my back, and you damn well know it, Morgan."

Morgan only nodded this time. He wasn't going to get anywhere arguing with Ball.

"Pull up here," Ball said, appearing to calm down a little. He and Morgan rode into the shade of an oak while the patrol passed by. Ball took a map from a leather holder and held it out to Morgan. "We're about here." A finger tapped the map. "The captain wants me to ride the perimeter—where we figure our area of responsibility ends—up through the Tangles, back to Stone Creek, then across to Little Trace and back home. On our right now, to the north, is Harry Hodges and his patrol, to the south the kid . . . shouldn't say that . . . Lieutenant Doran.

"As I said, we turn south at the Tangles—that's what they call the hills up beyond. A lot of dead wood and jumbled rocks. It's no place for a cavalry unit really. Break a horse's leg, ride into places you can hardly get out of."

"But it's a damn fine place for someone that's hiding out," Shelter suggested. "Panther or the raiders."

"That's right," Ball replied. "That's where I want you to go, Morgan, check it out up there. You even *smell* anything, you get your ass out and get back to the unit, you hear?"

"I hear you."

"No objection?" Ball asked with a thin smile.

"No, sir," Morgan answered honestly. He had no objection at all to riding into the Tangles. As near as he could tell, that was where Boomer indicated Pablo Ruiz was hiding out.

"Very good . . ." Ball hesitated, then turned his horse and heeled it out of there, riding toward the head of his column.

Morgan sat his pinto sucking at a tooth, looking at the land around him. It was interesting, very interesting. "How do you suppose something like that happens?" Shelter asked the pinto.

The map the army officer was carrying seemed to be accurate. But it didn't match worth a damn the map Shelter had taken from the courthouse. Without having the two side by side it wasn't easy to figure out which was wrong and by how much—but they didn't match. They just didn't.

65

Morgan started on, paying more attention now to the way the land fell, from time to time looking at his map. Of course much of this area hadn't been surveyed, and the mapmakers who had come in had very hastily done their work and scatted before the Indians could make maps on their hides. A lot of western maps were more guesswork than reality. Some of those had gotten a lot of would-be settlers and gold seekers killed.

Shelter knew of one case where a man in Philadelphia, wanting to make some money off the California gold rush, had decided to make up his own maps off existing ones and sell them to the travelers. Dry lakes weren't indicated that way—just as lakes. Western rivers, always disappointing to an Easterner, weren't indicated as seasonal either. Distance was subject to whim. The Rocky Mountains were molehills with hundreds of passes even in deepest winter. The ancient mapmakers had been no more fanciful than this Philadelphian. By rights he should have been hung for out-and-out murder, but he was never prosecuted.

The Tangles were on the map. Shelter found himself heading into an area that was nothing more or less than badlands. A devil's playground with gigantic boulders careening in all directions, with the remains of a dead forest choking off the bottoms and rising, broken battlements blocking out the sun.

No wonder Ball didn't want to bring his force in here. The opportunity for ambush was limitless. Maybe, Morgan thought, that's why he *did* want to send me.

He moved slowly through the corridors among the boulders, many of them house-sized and larger, the pinto picking its way over the white skeletons of trees.

Just what had happened here? An earthquake followed by a flood? The land was dead and empty. A lizard clinging to the face of a boulder reminded Shelter that it was the first living thing he had seen since entering the Tangles.

He kept looking upward as he rode through the cool shadows, the horse's hoofs whispering over the sandy bottom. He wanted to find a way to get to higher ground so that he could watch for Boomer.

She would probably be coming over the flat where Cooney's cabin was, but Morgan, turned around a little now, wasn't sure exactly where it was. He needed to be higher up to see.

He rode down a long corridor-like canyon where the black stone was polished as smooth as glass and then through a narrower canyon where water had honey-combed the walls so that it looked like Swiss cheese with thousands upon thousands of head-sized and smaller holes.

He still had not seen the tracks of another horse or of a man afoot in the Tangles, and that suited him just fine. Now he did find a way up, however. Just a spot where the wall of the canyon had broken down forming a ramp to the ridge fifty feet above him. Morgan swung down and led the pinto up the ramp, several times slipping, once almost losing the horse, before they clambered up and out of the canyon.

The breeze gusted over him up there, cooling his flesh. Morgan removed his hat, wiped his forehead, and slapped the Stetson back on. Looking to the east he searched the pine ridge there, expecting to see Boomer arrive from that direction if and when she did arrive.

In the meantime Shelter decided on a little more exploring.

There was another tier of rocks higher up. From there he thought he should be able to see out most of the Tangles and possibly even back to the Kennedy house along the Trace. Leaving the horse ground-hitched, he started up the rocks which stood gray and close together like massive tombstones.

The wind blasted against his body, chilling him. It would rain again, and soon, he thought. Morgan dragged himself up and onto the level ground above the rocks. There sand soil provided a tenuous life for clumps of salt grass and nopal cactus.

The flat, perhaps half a mile long, was crescent shaped, dotted with still other boulders and some dead timber. Morgan stood looking eastward, shading his eyes, and then started toward the north end of the crescent.

Boomer was there.

Her little boot tracks were clearly evident in the soil and Morgan's eyes lifted to the rocks ahead, an odd-shaped collection stacked like a kid's wooden blocks.

"Boomer!" he called out.

There was no answer. The wind whistled through the rocks. The badlands spread out for mile upon mile to his left. Far to the south he saw dust which he took for Ball's patrol. To the north there were storm clouds and a long green valley beyond the Tangles.

"Boomer!"

There was still no answer. He walked around the stacked boulders, following her tracks up an increasingly narrow trail. He had to put his belly to the stones and ease along sideways. Behind him the bluff fell away to the canyon floor. What in hell was she doing here? The

answer had to be that this was where Ruiz had holed up—
and it was a good place for it.

The rocks opened suddenly and Shelter found himself
facing a narrow cave. The lady was standing there, bent
over something dark and crumpled.

"Boomer?" Shelter said, and she turned and shot him.

6.

The flash from the rifle muzzle washed out the image of the girl in a blaze of fiery light and Morgan was punched backward, searing pain flooding his chest as he went over the rim and fell to the floor of the canyon below. His body thudded against the sandy earth, but he never felt it. He was unconscious long before he met the ground, spinning through a mind-born chasm much, much deeper than the gorge.

It was cold, very cold. Opening an eye Morgan saw the rain slanting down out of a cold sky. Water ran down his face and soaked through his clothing. He tried to move, but his body was a distant thing fighting against his mind.

He closed his eyes, seeing the same image over and over. The woman turning, the fiery blast, the pain and endless falling.

"Boomer . . . Boomer."

It was a hundred years before she answered, and when she did the rain had stopped. Morgan was looking up at darkness, not the darkness of a night sky, but a deeper, muskier darkness. It was Boomer who was bent over him, touching his face with a damp warm cloth.

"What'd you shoot me for?" Morgan asked from out

of the deep pit.

"You all right, Shell? God, I thought you were done."

"What'd you shoot me for?" he asked again.

"I didn't shoot you, big boy. I aim low, remember."

"Yeah, that's right . . ." He found her hand and squeezed it. Rolling his head to one side he saw a tiny fire beside which a man was sitting on his haunches.

"Who's that? The devil . . . ?"

He laughed a little and it hurt. Then he wasn't laughing or seeing anything, he was back in the deep pit fighting off swarms of flying pigs.

When he came around again it was lighter. He sat up and slapped at his holster. His Colt was there and he lay back, reassured. Pain throbbed in his shoulder. His head was being attacked by little men with big hammers.

"Come on, let's have some soup, " Boomer said. Shell opened one eye to peer at the redhead.

"What in hell happened?"

"Don't you know?" She half-sat him up, propped against a saddle and bedroll. The fire was still burning, but the man was gone. Now Morgan could see that he was in a small cave. Outside the sky had the dull glow of rain. "Where's the man? Who was that? Or was I dreaming?" Morgan asked before Boomer spooned a mouthful of beef soup into his mouth.

"Pablo Ruiz. He went out to scavenge some wood." She nudged him with the spoon. "Open up. You lost a lot of blood, you need to eat."

Morgan gently fingered the wound high up on the left side of his chest, just below the collarbone. "She nearly got me, didn't she?"

"Who?" Boomer asked, brushing a strand of red hair from her face.

71

"That's just it, I don't know. You know, at the Hawkins' place they found the tracks of a woman. A woman tried to ambush me not long ago—I thought it was you, as a matter of fact. Yesterday—was it yesterday?—I found some small bootprints. Thought they were yours. I followed them along and got shot."

"By a woman?"

"Unless I was dreaming."

"Funny—that's what Pablo said. I thought he was crazy."

"What do you mean, Boomer?"

"He said a woman was running the raiders. Said she was behind all of this."

"What else did he say?" Morgan asked, holding the soupspoon away from his mouth.

"I'll let him tell you. He'll be back soon. Meanwhile, damn you, eat!" Boomer Kennedy ordered. "You're lucky to be alive. Lucky I found you. I was heading toward Pablo's hideout—this cave—and there you were sprawled out on the sand. Damn you, I thought you were dead."

Then Boomer shut up and fed him silently until the soup was gone. By then Ruiz was back. He was wearing a poncho, soaking wet now, carrying a bundle of dry wood snapped off the dead trees below. He appeared to be old, very old, but his hair was jet black, his eyes clear and alert. His movements were those of a younger man. His face was craggy, seamed, dark.

He dropped the wood by the fire, glanced at Shelter and Boomer but said nothing.

"Pablo?" Boomer said, and the eyes returned to them.

"Yes?"

72

"This is the man I was telling you about. He wants to talk to you about what you saw."

Pablo shrugged, placed a few sticks on the fire, and shuffled over to where Morgan sat. It wasn't going to be easy. Pablo didn't like talking much.

"You were at the Collins' place when the raiders hit, weren't you, Pablo?" Morgan asked.

The Indian looked as if he thought he were being accused of a crime. "Just sleeping. In the loft."

"But you saw them?"

"I saw them." Morgan waited but that was it. Everything was going to have to be pried out of the man.

"Soldiers?"

"I saw some men in army uniforms," Ruiz said. "I saw some men in no uniforms. I saw some Indians. Cheyenne."

Riding together? The idea seemed preposterous. Maybe that was why Ruiz hadn't gotten a good hearing in Rosalia. "Indians and soldiers together?"

"I saw this, yes. I did not say soldiers. I said men in army uniforms."

"You don't think they were soldiers, then."

"I don't know. They rode all sorts of horses."

Morgan knew what Ruiz meant. The army used bay horses exclusively for the enlisted ranks, of a standard size. Although an officer could buy and ride any color mount he wished, you weren't going to see enlisted men on paint ponies or roans or blacks.

Shelter thought that over. Men impersonating soldiers? Why ride with renegade Cheyenne anyway? It was a wonder any Cheyenne—Panther included—would agree to that. They'd be more likely to kill the whites out

73

of hand than to form a pact.

"The men in uniform, they couldn't have been Indians too?"

"Short hair. I know the way they ride," Ruiz said as if insulted.

"All right. Did you see anything else?"

"Just the woman."

The *woman*. She was back again. It was beyond doubting now: there was a woman involved in this somehow.

"What did you see of her? What did she look like?" Morgan wanted to know.

Pablo shrugged. Maybe he was past the age where it mattered what a woman looked like. "Small, like her," he said, nodding at Boomer. "Maybe black hair."

That was it. A small woman, maybe with black hair. And a murderous appetite. Ruiz knew a little more and he volunteered this information.

"I saw them again," he told Shelter. "They were riding north. To a place I know. Old rancheria. They use the Tangles a lot. They know nobody can follow an Indian through the Tangles. The army can't, the law can't."

"But you can."

Ruiz allowed himself a little smile. "I can follow anyone anywhere."

"Where is this place?" Boomer asked. "I've never heard of it."

"No whites go there. Now, some do. Thirty miles maybe. Where the Tangles meet the little creek called Bear Creek. Once I think a Frenchman had a trading post there. He was killed. This was long ago, maybe twenty years. Now it is the place where the raiders live."

"Would you show it to me?" Morgan asked.

74

Ruiz hesitated. "No," he said at last. "I don't want to go there. I don't want to die."

"Will you at least sketch out a little map?" Morgan asked.

"Yes," he said, "I will do that."

Shelter pulled out the map he had taken from the courthouse. Ruiz sat staring at it for a long moment. "This is wrong," he said at last.

"I know it is."

Boomer didn't know what they were talking about. "What's wrong?" she wanted to know.

"The map doesn't match the geography around here. I noticed that a time back. Somebody botched the job."

Boomer didn't attach any significance to that. "You know, another ranch was hit last night."

"Bad?"

"It was the Grant place. Seven sons and the old man, it seems they fought them off. Just lost the outbuildings and some livestock."

"I don't like any of this," Shelter said. "What can anyone do to hold the raiders off if the army is on their side?"

"You believe they are?"

"I just don't know."

"What do we do now?" Boomer asked.

"*We*, lady, don't do anything."

"Uh-oh," Boomer said, "you've got ideas, don't you?"

"Maybe."

She shook her head. "You've got a bullet hole in you, mister. You're not going to do anything for a long while."

"A day or two, I'd say." Morgan answered. Boomer frowned.

"And then what?" she asked.

75

"Why, then I'm going to go out to the outlaw camp and have a look around."

"What's the matter with you! Did you hit your head when you fell, Shelter Morgan? Those people know who you are."

"No, they don't. They might think they do, but they don't."

"Besides, just anyone who goes around is going to be shot on sight, and you know it."

"I'll come up with some story."

Boomer sighed. "Show me the story that'll stop a bullet."

"You worry too much."

"You trust this Captain Shirke, don't you? Why don't you report what you know to him. Let the army handle it."

"They haven't done a real good job of that so far, have they? I think I trust Shirke, I don't know. I don't know who to trust just now. Besides, what do I really have to report? That I think I know where the raiders are. That's it."

"It should be enough. Are you plain nuts or is someone paying you enough to make you commit suicide in the line of duty?"

"I don't like these people, Boomer," Shelter said seriously. "I don't like raiders coming in the middle of the night to slaughter innocent people in their sleep, to destroy everything they've worked for."

"A white knight," Boomer said with disgust.

"Not exactly," Shell grinned. "But I seem to be about all the people along the Little Trace have."

The rain fell steadily for the next two days. Morgan slept a lot, but whenever he opened his eyes Boomer

76

seemed to be there, watching. "Why don't you go home, lady? Your father will be wondering where you are."

"See, Pablo, I told you. I *have* been home, Shell. You were out for forty-eight hours the first time you went to sleep."

"You should have stayed home then," Morgan said grumpily. There was pain, stiffness, and a lot of itching under his bandages.

"And let you take care of yourself, I suppose," Boomer said.

"Well . . ." Morgan grinned and scratched his head. "Got any real food to eat, Boomer?"

"Smoked venison. I shot it, Pablo butchered it."

"I have corn cakes," Ruiz volunteered.

It was the best meal Morgan had had in his life. His body was craving food and he gorged himself, sitting back only when he couldn't stuff another mouthful down.

"Hope you don't eat like that all the time," Boomer said, taking his tin plate away. When she looked back Morgan was on his feet. "Now what do you think you're doing!"

"Just getting up. You should be happy about it, Boomer. You don't want to take care of a man who's flat on his back for long."

"I'd feel better about it if your legs weren't wobbling," Boomer answered.

She was right. Shell took careful, small steps to the mouth of the cave to stand looking down at the Tangles, still shrouded in mist. The breeze that met him was cool, damp, clean. He was upright, his belly was full. The world was good.

"Where's my horse, Boomer?" he asked.

"What're you going to do, go riding out?"

"Just wondering."

"I've got it up on top of the mesa. I don't think you should have a horse, mister, the way you keep track of that one."

"Next time I get shot maybe it'll kill me and I won't have to hear a woman's lecturing," Morgan said, but he was smiling and he hobbled over to Boomer, gathering her in his arm. The left he kept dangling, lifting it hurt like hell. "Feels good having you against me," Shelter said, kissing the top of her head. "Damn nice."

She could feel the stirring in his groin and she shook her head. "I guess you *are* getting better."

"Want me to show you?"

She nodded toward Pablo, who was stoking the fire as if it held all of his interest.

"We'll see—another time," Boomer answered, pushing him away gently.

After all the sleeping he had done Morgan still felt weary. He slept again and then rose to eat again, as voraciously as before. Boomer was still there, hovering over him.

Again he suggested, "You ought to go on home, lady."

"Think you can take care of yourself, do you?"

"I can. This laying around is starting to get to me anyway. It's time I did something."

"Like go back to the fort," Boomer said sternly.

"Sure."

"You don't still have that crazy idea about going up to the outlaw camp."

Morgan just looked at her and she spun away in disgust. "Of all the hard-headed men I've run into, you win the grand prize, Morgan! It's plain stupid."

"As bad as you, huh?"

78

"What are you talking about?" Boomer asked, her eyes narrowing.

"You don't belong out here either. You belong in Rosalia, and you know it."

"I can't leave Dad. I can't just walk away from things, Shelter."

"Neither can I," he answered quietly.

In the morning Boomer was gone. So was Ruiz, although he had left a sack of supplies and a canteen for Shelter. He was on his own again. Good, that was the way he wanted it, the way it had to be just now. Checking out his rifle and its loads, Morgan started out into the gray morning, saddlebags over his shoulder.

The paint was picketed in some long grass among the pines. It lifted its head at Shelter's approach, apparently weary itself of enforced inactivity. Boomer had left Shell's saddle under a tarp and he smoothed the blanket, swung the old Texas-rigged saddle up, and cinched down.

Then he was aboard, riding slowly north, his eyes combing the Tangles below, wondering just what he was riding into.

He found a break in the bluff and went again to the sandy bottom of the mazelike canyon. The wind was cold, the skies clotted with shifting clouds. Morgan was starting to see tracks.

In the sand they were indistinct, but there were a lot of them. Men riding north into the badlands, and there was only one place to go out there. There would be watchers in the rocks ahead. It was time to stop and think about just getting the hell out of there; but Shelter had already decided. He wanted to find the outlaw camp and discover just what in hell was going on in Dakota.

And he wanted to see the lady who was behind all of

this, find out just what drove her.

By evening he was twenty more miles into the badlands, a little tired due to his wound, and a little more uneasy. He wanted high ground now and found a place the horse could climb as the sunset stained the sky deep red and purple.

From above he could see for miles more. The badlands extended for another ten miles or so and then gradually broke off, becoming buffalo prairie to the north. There was timber to the west on the low hills, and directly ahead was the light of a pair of campfires.

Morgan swung down from the pinto's back and crouched, watching the fires, eventually spotting a third and then a fourth fire as the sky dimmed and his eyes adjusted. He thought he could make out a long low building, but it was in the hollow and in shadow and he couldn't be sure. Yet that had to be it, the outlaw haven.

He waited until it was nearly full dark, the sun just a memory in orange against the high clouds, before he started nearer, meaning to have his look.

He ran into the three outlaws in the canyon bottom.

Coming out of a feeder canyon he practically rode into them. He heard hammers drawn back in the darkness and said, "Easy, boys, I'm with you."

"Who are you," one of them asked.

"Martin." Why not? It was a good enough name and a common enough one, first or last name. It was the first one that popped into Morgan's mind anyway. His own hand had slipped to the butt of his holstered Colt and closed over the walnut grips.

"We thought you was an Indian or a soldier."

Shelter relaxed just a hair. "Not guilty of either." He tried to get a handle on this and thought he had it suddenly. "Who are you boys supposed to report to?"

"Drake."

"Me too," Morgan said. He had guessed right. These three hadn't shot him on the spot. They were new men, reinforcements drifting in to the raider camp.

"You don't know him?" a second raider asked suspiciously.

"No. You boys pass a cavalry patrol?"

"Yeah. Down south. We rode wide."

"Wish we would have. They got Sol and Tanner."

"Thought the army wouldn't come near this place."

"That's what I thought," Morgan said. Hell, it appeared the army ran this place. He had trapped himself into something now. Meaning only to have a look at the camp he had fallen in with three more raiders. There was only one way to go—straight ahead. "Anyone got a bottle?" he asked.

"I got a flask."

It was handed over to Shelter who took only a small drink and handed it back, wiping his mouth. "Where you boys up from?"

"Kansas, you?"

"Colorado. Hope this thing works out. Last job I had we got shot up, run out, and fired." He rubbed his arm. "I still got a hole in me."

"And you're comin' back for more."

"Got to make a living. Been trying since the war to figure out some other way," Shelter said, "But it keeps coming back to a gun."

"What side was you on?" one of the outlaws asked. Morgan knew that the Tennessee accent was still there no matter what. There was no sense denying it.

"Gray," he answered.

"We were on both sides," the outlaw said with a loud guffaw. "Kansas was the only place to make a profit in the war."

That was enough to turn Morgan against these three. A man believed in something and he fought. Maybe he just got caught up in something and he fought. But war's not the place to set out to make a profit.

"Maybe we'll make us a little here," Shelter said.

"Maybe so, Martin. You know what the whole scoop is?"

"Not really. I was thinking there may be a way to get more than fighting wages, though. With the four of us . . . maybe."

The outlaw agreed. "Maybe so. I'm Dent, this is Howard Bishop, and the skinny one's Carl Pierce." They shook hands all around, firm handshakes that meant nothing. These men would kill their grandmothers without blinking. They saw Morgan as a potential ally, that was all. The trick was to keep them thinking that way.

It might not last long. Only until Shelter rode into the raiders' camp and met someone he knew all too well. For now it would have to do to keep him alive another few hours.

He started north again with the three hired guns at his back.

7.

There wasn't anything to it. The four new guns rode into the raider camp and were met by a man named Foley, a long-jawed whiskered gunny with two silver-mounted Colts and the temper of a rattler.

"We wanted to see the boss, Drake," Dent said. Morgan sat back and allowed Dent to take charge.

"Well, you're not seeing Drake. There's the bunkhouse. Make your beds or get out," Foley said.

"I guess we'll make our beds," Dent said very slowly. He didn't like being bullied obviously, especially not in front of his friends. "But we didn't ride from Kansas to be stiffed."

"You men are a dozen to a dime," Foley said. "You don't like it, ride out. Or try," he added nastily.

Dent wanted to say something, but he didn't. He jerked his horse's head around and rode to the long log bunkhouse, the others following. Inside, Shelter got his first good look at the gunmen.

Able Dent was lean, blond, with a long jagged scar across his cheek. Bishop was heavy, dark, and fat-lipped. Carl Pierce looked like a kid with his skinny build and freckled face, but he was carrying a lot of notches on his gun butts. Morgan didn't care for a one of them. Nevertheless, they were all he had for cover.

"Bastard! Talking to me like that!" Dent said, throwing his bedroll onto his bunk.

"Just a paper gunny," Morgan said.

"He got here first," Bishop put in. "Big man because of it. Down in Lawrence we would have flattened him out and jerked him."

Shelter picked out an empty bunk and stretched out on it. "I hear we're working with Indians on this job. What do you think of that?" he asked.

"Indians? Don't know a thing about it."

"I never heard that," Howard Bishop said.

Morgan gave it up. These three knew about as much as he did about how things worked around here. A couple of men wandered in. No one was introduced, no one spoke. A silent poker game started up at the far end of the barracks.

After an hour or so Shelter got up, yawned, and said, "I'm going out for some air."

Pierce glanced at him. No one said anything. Outside it was starry to the south, heaped with clouds to the north. A cold wind drifted across the camp. Morgan started a slow tour of the place. There were two dozen or so men in camp, most of them eating around the campfires or drinking coffee. No one challenged his right to be there.

He saw no soldiers, no Indians. There was another bunkhouse across the camp, but there were no lights on in it, and it was presumably empty.

He saw the ruins of an old stone building—the Frenchman's trading post, he decided—and back up in the trees another structure where lights were blazing. He started that way.

Walking through the pines his boots made no sound against the needles littering the ground. The house was two stories high. The bottom floor was old stone like the trading post, the top floor added on more recently was of lumber, unpainted.

The guard stepped out from behind a tree and lowered his rifle at Shelter's belly.

"What are you doing up here, friend?"

"Walking around."

"You're walking the wrong way," the short man in the open rain slicker said.

"Sorry, just rode in tonight. Nobody told me a thing."

"Just rode in, did you?" The guard peered at Morgan out of the darkness. "Keep those hands high, why don't you?" He moved nearer and in a quick movement lifted Shell's Colt.

"What's the trouble?" Shelter asked. "I was just taking a look around."

"The trouble is, I don't know you, friend. Let's go— you wanted to see the big house, let's have a closer look."

Morgan went ahead of the guard, his hands still raised. He thought about trying to disarm the rifle-wielding mercenary but that would get him nowhere. Except maybe dead. He had started this bluff, now he had to work his way through it, hoping that he didn't run into someone at the house he didn't want to see.

Someone in a blue uniform.

They marched right up to the front door, treading on sagging, squeaky steps past another guard who sat sagging in a tilted wooden chair.

"Gant inside?"

The other guard nodded. Shelter was pushed ahead to open the bleak gray plank door and step into something

85

totally unexpected. The old Frenchman's house had been paneled and carpeted. White light leaked out into the corridor. Beyond a door Shelter could have sworn he heard the sounds of crystal and cutlery.

"Turn right," his guide directed, and Morgan walked down a short corridor to a small room that was painted a flat green, furnished only with a puncheon table and chair. A broken-nosed, hard-eyed man sat at the table, a bottle of whiskey in front of him. He looked up sharply as Morgan was ushered into the room.

"What've you got, Tom?"

"I don't know, Mr Gant. Just found this fellow roving around a little too near the house."

"Didn't anyone ever tell you to stay away from this house, mister?" Gant asked. He reached for his bottle of whiskey and leaned back in his chair.

"Says he just got here tonight," the guard said.

"That right?"

"I been sitting a horse all day," Shelter said. "I just wanted to stretch my legs out. Nobody told me a thing."

"What's your name?"

"Martin. Glen Martin."

"Where you from, Martin?"

"He rode in with the boys from Kansas, the ones Shaw recruited," the guard said. Morgan hoped his gratitude didn't show.

"Shaw sent us up. We were down in Lawrence waiting for the law to show up. This seemed like a better deal. Me, Dent, Bishop, and Pierce came on up. What's the matter, don't you want soldiers?"

Gant was staring at both of them equally hard. The guard, Tom, had said one word too many when he mentioned Shaw's name. "Damn Foley," is what Gant finally said. "He's supposed to warn the new men about coming around."

"He was more concerned with impressing Dent that he was boss," Shelter said.

"Yeah. That's Foley." Gant took a drink from his whiskey bottle while Tom watched hopefully. "All right. Take him back, Tom. You stay away from the big house, understand, Martin?"

"Sure, I understand. Anything goes with me. I'm just here for wages—but somebody's got to tell me, you know."

"You've been told now."

The door behind Shelter opened and he half-turned.

"Gant, I want—" the voice broke off. Morgan was just staring. It was a woman, and not an ordinary-looking woman. Five foot two maybe, with slashing dark eyes and black hair pinned up and decorated with a silver something. She wore a beaded white dress wrapped around a curving little body. The breasts were creamy and firm, pushing up from the top of the dress. "Have we met?" the lady asked.

"He just got here, Mizz Drake," Gant said.

"I could have sworn . . ." the lady was still looking at the lean, blue-eyed man before her. There was no objection to what she saw in her eyes, only puzzlement.

Sure they'd met before—when she put that bullet through Morgan's shoulder. This was the boss lady, Drake. And damn it all if she wasn't the most beautiful woman Shelter had ever seen off a stage.

There was something of a tease about her full lips, something of a sensual woman in her eyes, but there was nothing at all to suggest she was a cold-blooded killer. Her little pink ears and sleek neck, the soft rising and falling of her breasts, were all extraordinarily feminine and soft. You wouldn't imagine her behind the sights of a Winchester, but that was where Shelter had seen her the last time they'd met.

It had been dark in the cave and she had turned swiftly, firing before she had time to examine her target. Still there was some image lurking in the back of her skull, some memory of having seen Shelter before.

And if she dredged it up and remembered . . . Shelter beat her to it. "You ever go out hunting, miss?"

"Sometimes . . . Oh, no!" She laughed out loud.

"Yeah," Morgan smiled. He touched his shoulder. "Right through there."

"What is this?" Gant asked suspiciously.

"I was down in the Tangles and someone came up behind me. I'm afraid it was Mr. Martin. I shot him."

"Blew me right off the cliff," Shelter said.

"One of my own men!"

She was smiling, Gant wasn't. Morgan said, "It was starting to rain. We were looking for a place to hole up. Didn't expect to run into a she-lion in that cave."

The lady laughed and Morgan figured he should join in. He was hoping she didn't recall sniping at him near the Hawkins' house. But that had been at long distance and she couldn't possibly have recognized him on that day.

Or so he hoped.

"It looks like I owe you something, Mr. Martin," the lady said.

"I just want wages, Miss Drake."

"Donna," she suggested. "You can call me Donna." She stuck out a little white hand which had a firmer grip

88

than Morgan had expected.

"I'd be pleasured, Miss . . . Donna."

"Southerner?" she asked, tilting her head.

"Tennessee."

"War experience?"

"Yes."

"How much?" she inquired with interest.

"Too much. Nearly five years—not counting the prison time I did afterward. They nailed me for a spy."

"You were an officer?"

"I went in as a private. Came out a captain," Shell acknowledged. All of that was true and the lady seemed more and more interested.

In several ways.

"Maybe we can use Mr. Martin as more than just a soldier," Donna Drake suggested. "We lost Campbell at the Grant place, didn't we?"

"We don't hardly know this man," the raider objected.

"No." She eyed Shelter more closely and then smiled again, and it was a smile deep with expectation and sexual anticipation. "But maybe we can get to know him a lot better."

Morgan was handed his gun at Donna's instruction and shown the door. The woman's eyes followed him all the way out. Good. He had made a friend, and maybe an enemy. Gant didn't seem to think much of taking a new man in that quickly.

Back at the barracks nothing had changed, except a few more men had drifted in from somewhere.

"Where you been?" Dent demanded.

Morgan sat on the bunk opposite, facing the hired gun. "Oh, they gave me some trouble out there. That Foley

89

has gone carrying stories to the boss."

"What kind of stories?" Howard Bishop asked suspiciously, his fat lips barely moving.

"I'm not sure. As it turned out I was able to cover for you. Happens I know the boss—never realized it. She asked me if you boys were all right and I said sure, I'd known you down in Kansas. We worked together down there, rode all the way up together. Foley was just making trouble. Stick to that if anyone asks you."

"Sure. Appreciate it, Martin."

"*She?*" Carl Pierce said. He had caught it. "You mean to tell me this outfit is being ramrodded by a woman?"

"It sure is, but she's an exception. Believe me. Donna knows what she's up to."

"How'd you meet this lady?" a still-suspicious Dent asked.

"Believe it or not," Morgan said, stretching out, tugging his hat down over his face, "we used to go shooting together."

With Shelter as the target.

There wasn't any more discussion except for some muttering about what a bastard Foley was. Morgan lay there silently, not sleeping. He was trying his best to cover his butt at both ends, but how long that would work he couldn't be sure.

There were a lot of empty bunks around and Shell figured some of the gang was out on a raid that night. Wearing army uniforms? Or *were* they army? If someone from the post showed up, he was a goner. Outside of that he was reasonably unknown in the territory. Yet, even if his masquerade held up, what in hell was he going to be able to do to stop these killers? Without a sense of security he finally managed to doze off, dreaming of dark-

90

haired women with lush naked bodies and thundering guns.

Before dawn they were up and stirring. Men, muttering under their breath, moved through the cold of morning toward the door, buckling on their guns, snatching up rifles.

Foley and Gant were outside as they emerged into the gray light. Nothing was said, but they took special notice of Morgan and his adopted gang.

"Bastard's holding a grudge," Howard Bishop decided.

"If they don't want me, I'll ride out," Pierce said, although the truth was that they were on the run and out of places to ride to, out of work if this didn't go through.

They rambled after the rest of the warriors, heading for a shack where somebody was cooking something and boiling coffee. Shelter was still interested in covering himself. He asked, "How much did Shaw give you boys when he recruited you anyway?"

"Fifty bucks, gold money," Dent said.

Shelter just grunted, leaving the other three to wonder if they had gotten beaten out of something. Morgan just wanted to know in case someone asked *him*.

He took a rough count of the men in camp and multiplied by fifty—someone was playing for big stakes here. There was a lot of gold sunk into this private army.

Breakfast was tasteless cornbread and beef and gravy served with black coffee. Morgan didn't waste much time over it. He went back outside while dawn colors still hung in the morning sky. Spying Foley, he walked over to the outlaw foreman.

"What do you want me to do today?" he asked.

Foley's snake eyes flickered and he spat a stream of tobacco out. "Nothin'. Why?"

"I hate taking money for nothing," Shelter answered. "Say, Foley—it seems that Dent and them got something against you. I just wanted to let you know it don't go for me. I'm here for wages. You're the boss as far as I'm concerned."

Foley's expression didn't change, but he seemed vaguely pleased with having someone tell him he was the boss gun. "All right. I'll mark that down, Martin."

Shelter nodded and turned away. He nearly walked into Dent and Bishop who was picking his teeth with a penknife. "What did the big man want?" Dent asked.

"Just told me to watch my butt or he'd have it," Shelter said, glancing back. "I guess we got started on the wrong foot."

"Let's hear him tell me that," Dent said, starting forward, but Shelter grabbed his arm. "They got too many guns, Dent. Let it lay. It'll blow over."

"Yeah." Dent had to take several deep breaths to calm himself. "I just don't like that weasel."

"His time'll come," Shelter said with a wink. Then he walked on, leaving his "friends" to stew.

He saw Tom, but the guard didn't say anything to him as he walked on toward the other bunkhouse, kicking at pine cones. The bunkhouse, beneath the pines, was empty, but it hadn't been for long. The earth in front of it had been packed hard by boots and horses' hoofs. Glancing back Morgan saw no one, so he went in.

It was set up like the other bunkhouse. Unmade beds along each wall, here and there a sock or dirty shirt. Shelter looked outside once more, saw no one, and went through the building a little more carefully. He found only one thing of interest.

The closet at the end of the bunkhouse was filled with

cavalry uniforms.

He shuffled through them. Authentic and complete down to the boots. His mouth was tight as he slammed the closet door and turned back.

Tom was there with his rifle.

"You. Let's get going. Someone wants to talk to you up at the big house."

8.

Up the front porch past a different sleepy guard and into the familiar corridor Shelter led Tom and his Winchester. He started to turn toward the room where Gant had interviewed him, but Tom stopped him.

"Not that way, straight ahead."

Morgan did as he was told. His belly was drawn up tight, his pulse racing although his movements were slow and catlike. He had bought it now. Tom had caught him snooping where he didn't belong. He still had his Colt, but how in hell did you shoot your way past thirty armed men?

At the end of the corridor they turned left, passing a huge dining room where a long table was set with linen and silver, and approached a carved mahogany door.

"Right here," Tom said. Morgan stopped and waited while his guide knocked on the heavy door.

Inside, the room was white marble and dark wood. Someone was planning on staying here a long time. Probably the little dark-eyed woman behind the carved desk. She rose and said, "That's all, Tom."

He objected, "Gant said—"

"That's all, Tom." For the first time Morgan saw the

hardness in those eyes and sensed the power behind the slender woman.

"Yes, Miss Drake," he said and left, making sure the door only whispered shut.

"Sit down," the lady invited and Morgan did. "Would you like a cigar, Glen?"

"No thanks," the man known as Glen Martin said, crossing his legs as he leaned back in a green leather chair.

"You were looking around the ranch again, I hear," Donna Drake said.

"That's right. Nothing else to do. Foley said he didn't have any work for me. I wanted to get the layout down."

"Why?" She was playing with a silver paper knife. Her eyes were halfway between their alluring softness and the hard businesslike stare she had given Tom. Morgan realized he wasn't playing with a fool. The answer had to be good.

"The more I know, the better off I am. I hear the army prowls this area. If there's a war, I want to know which way to go."

"You don't have to worry about the army," Donna said.

"No?"

"No."

"How about the Indians? I hear a renegade named Panther is roaming the Tangles too."

She laughed harshly. "You know a hell of a lot for a man who just rode in."

"I ask questions," Morgan said. "It keeps me alive. Lady, I've been in a war of one sort or the other for the last ten years. There's three things I rely on: my own skill with arms, luck, and intelligence. What I don't know can

95

kill me."

"It can work the other way," the lady said.

She stood, walked around the desk, and perched on it. She wore a divided riding skirt of off-green and a white blouse that fit the curves of her breasts nicely.

She seemed to be thinking deeply as she studied her hands. Morgan looked around the rest of the room, seeing the small marble statues of a shepherd and a nymph, the crossed sabers, the white lace curtains.

And the map.

On Donna's wall was a huge map of the territory perhaps four feet by three. It was an old map, but well-preserved. And it was accurate in every detail, much more accurate than the map from the courthouse. It didn't take more than a glance to see that.

"You interested in maps?" Donna asked, following his eyes.

"I told you—I like to know what's going on," Shelter answered.

"I think you do," she said, "more than you let on."

"Do you?" Morgan felt the tightness in his belly again. He hoped it didn't show on his face.

"Yes. Men come and go here. You're different. Always looking. Why is that?"

"I told you. Besides, wages are fine, but where there's an operation of this size something big is up for grabs. Maybe I've been working for wages too long."

"Looking for the main chance?"

"Who isn't?"

The lady laughed. She rose, and with her back to Shelter asked abruptly, "What's your real name?"

"What's yours?" he shot back, and apparently that

tactic worked. The lady laughed again.

"Donna, just Donna," she said, turning back toward him. "Mr. Martin, I think we're going to get along fine. I hope so," she said, the tone of her voice changing just a little, that power coming back into it. "Maybe wages won't be the end of it. We'll see."

"Mind telling me now exactly what's going on?" Morgan asked.

"What did Shaw tell you?"

"Shaw told us, 'Here's fifty bucks gold, ride north.'"

There was a knock on the doorframe and Gant came in, looking smug and grim. He walked to the lady's desk and tossed something on it. "Found it in his saddlebags," the gunman said.

Donna reached back and picked it up. The courthouse map. Unfolding it she studied it, smiling to herself. "You know quite a bit more than you're telling, obviously, Glen."

"Why? I got the map to find my way around."

"Sure." The lady looked at Gant. "That'll be all, Willis."

"But, Mizz Drake . . ."

"That's all!" she repeated. Her voice was low, but there was no mistaking the power behind her words. Fuming, Gant left, glancing once at Morgan.

"You interest me very much," Donna Drake said.

"You interest me," Shell answered, letting his words take on another meaning as his eyes swept up her body.

"You know that's not what I meant." Still she smiled, pleased by his attention. "The map. The wandering around you've been doing. Why were you in the other bunkhouse anyway, Glen Martin?"

"Seeing what was what, if they had it any better."

"Really." She wasn't much convinced. "And why the map?"

"I told you. You don't come into strange territory and find your way easily."

"I thought Shaw gave everyone a map," the woman said with a brief, bright smile.

"I never got one."

"This one couldn't have helped much," she said tapping it with her finger.

"I noticed that. It's cockeyed," Shelter said with a shrug. He smiled, but he was worried, very worried. The lady wasn't just fencing with words, she was turning something around in that sharp little mind of hers, measuring Shelter. If things went wrong she wasn't above having him killed and he knew it.

"You said you wanted to know what was going on up here—I think you already know, Mr. Martin."

"I just know something's brewing. There's a lot of guns in this camp. That means the stakes are big. There's a lot of strange stories going around the territory. Some of them don't make much sense. You"—he looked around the room—"you're planning on staying on for a long time, it seems."

"What else have you deduced?" she asked, rising to stand over him. Now Morgan saw the little silver derringer at the back of her waist. Apparently the lady took no chances.

"Nothing but what I said. There's something big going on, and maybe a chance to make more than just wages. I'm looking for something, Donna, something to hook onto. I can't be just a hired hand forever."

She turned away and with her back to Shelter asked, "What do you think of Gant and Foley?"

"Gant's a drunk with a mean streak, Foley alienates the men with his badgering. Neither strikes me as a warrior. Just street thugs."

"I'm afraid you're right," she said. "I'm looking for a general. All I get is more soldiers. I spotted something in you right off. That's why I asked you about your army experience."

"Oh?" Shelter tried to keep his voice calm. This could be just what he was looking for—or it could be a deadly trap.

"It all goes back to the maps," she said, turning to face him and perch on the desktop again. "It's no mistake that the official map of the area is wrong. It was planned that way."

"By who?"

"By myself and another person."

"Who?"

"Don't ask so many questions, Martin."

"Sorry, I told you I like to know the setup when I work."

"Yes." She drew out the word and rolled it off her tongue thoughtfully. "Anyway, the surveying was intentionally botched. The territory was just opening up to white settlers and we wanted to be first. If you look at your map and then at mine, you'll see exactly what was done. The country between the Little Trace and the mountains was shrunk down. Actually, if you care, there's a million acres missing."

Shelter, looking at the big wall map, could see that the lady was exactly right. And if she said it was a million acres, she was probably right about that too.

"No one was supposed to move in here until April. But the word got out and a few dozen ranchers crept in early, some as much as a year early."

"And set up on the land you had pegged for yourself."

"Yes, the greedy bastards," she said without intended irony. "Just how could we get rid of them? If we argued that they were on the wrong land the manipulation of the survey would come out. And it seemed very likely that no court would evict them from open land which they'd proved up on. Not to hand it back to us."

"You have title to the land, but it doesn't exist legally."

She smiled, "Complicated, isn't it? Yes, we set the land aside as a sort of invisible empire, our private reservation. It's much cheaper to buy what looks to be a few thousand acres than a million—besides, they have some ridiculous restriction on how much land a private party can buy."

"One day they'll find out."

"Yes, after the next survey which might be ten or twenty years off. But by then we'll have tenure and nobody will move us off. If it happens, we'll spread some money around."

The lady was smart, too smart by half. She kept saying "we"—just who was in this with her?

"The problem was to move the ranchers off without seeming to be involved."

"Yes. They have to quit their land."

Shelter weighed his next words carefully. He was giving away a little too much, maybe, but he had to know. "You decided to use the Indians. Panther's renegades."

100

She laughed out loud. Donna just threw back her head and laughed long and hard. "Oh, Martin, you do get around."

"I told you . . ."

"Yes, I know, you want to know what you're into. All right, we told Panther that we were going to give him half the land. He doesn't trust us, but that's all right for now. He fights with us and we need all the help we can get. If nothing else he can distract the army—not that they seem to know what direction they're going in anyway."

"Folks in Rosalia and along the Trace seem to think soldiers have been involved."

"Do they now?" she asked, more subdued now. "I take it you saw the uniforms in the barracks. Come on, Martin, I'm no fool."

"I saw them. Where did they come from?"

"Sources. Never mind. I don't mind telling you what you need to know, but you don't need to know it all."

"There *are* soldiers involved, then."

"Never mind," she snapped. "I've told you all I'm going to. Probably too much, but I like you and I think we can use you. There have been too many botched jobs. It comes from sending out a mob instead of an organized army. Time is important here. We've got to move the settlers and move them fast."

"Blame it on the Indians and then move in yourself. And the army takes care of Panther after someone tips them off where his main camp is."

She was surprised this time. "You're very clever, Martin. I hope not too clever."

"All right. I can guess with anyone once I've been given something to work with." He shrugged deeply.

"You've told me all I need to know. The only thing that puzzles me is *why*. I'm new around here. True, I can help you with your little war, but you didn't have to tell me anything really. Why did you?"

"Because it doesn't matter, Glen Martin. If you're not who I think you are, if you get out of line, I'll simply have you killed."

The lady said it without emotion, and that's the way it would be done if Shelter was fingered—without emotion, coldly, maybe a little too slowly.

Donna rose from her perch and crossed to him. She bent her head low and kissed him hotly, almost savagely, her tongue forcing its way into his mouth. When she stepped back she was breathing roughly. "Don't let me down," she warned him. "Just don't let me down."

She stepped out into the hall and called for Gant. "Come to dinner tonight," she told Shelter while she waited for her lieutenant. "I'll have a suit laid out for you. You're moving from the bunkhouse up to here. Gant will show you your room. Gant!"

He appeared rubbing a whiskered jaw, reeking of raw whiskey.

"Yeah?"

"Martin's in charge of field forces. Fill him in."

"He's *what?* Your brother won't like this . . ."

"Shut up! He's in charge. Tell Foley and Carlos when Carlos comes back in."

Gant's glazed eyes fixed themselves on Morgan. Slowly he nodded. "Whatever you say, Mizz Drake."

"That's right, Willis, don't forget it. Whatever I say!" Gant stumped off and she turned back to Shelter with a heated smile. "Don't forget, dinner tonight."

"Whatever you say," Morgan said, grinning. He rose, looped an arm around her waist, and kissed her again, bruising her lips against her teeth. The woman liked it hard, it seemed.

Her finger traced the contours of his lips as she drew away. "God, big man, I hope I'm not making a mistake with you. I'd hate like hell to have to kill you."

Yeah. Morgan wasn't too crazy about the idea himself. He still couldn't quite figure the lady out. Was she just stringing him along? She didn't seem the sort to hand it all out on the limb out of passion, handing over the keys to the operation to a near stranger.

But you never knew—a man or a woman will do nearly anything once that itch creeps down to the groin.

It still could be a game. The lady had the instincts of a black widow, and maybe that was it. Love him and then kill him. Suck his insides out.

Morgan went out into the yard and looked around the camp. There was no way a man was going to walk out of there if the boss lady didn't want him to. Maybe it wasn't such a big risk after all.

Shell started across the grassy yard toward the bunkhouse.

Dent, Bishop, and Pierce were hanging around the bunkhouse steps. "Where you been?" Dent asked.

"Trying to find out what was going on, when we were going to get to work."

Morgan propped a boot up on the bunkhouse step and broke out his cigar, lighting it. "Learn anything?" Carl Pierce asked.

"Not much. But it turns out I know the boss. I've got myself a promotion, and you boys are going along with me."

"What are you talking about?"

"Just what I said. You don't pay any attention to Foley or anyone else starting now. Just to me, and you boys are my right hand."

Bishop blinked, and sucked at his fat lower lip. "Sounds good. Are you ready to prove it?"

"If I have to. Why?"

"That's just it—you have to," Bishop said, and he lifted his eyebrows meaningfully. Morgan turned to find the long-jawed Foley, his twin Colts low on his hips, watching him.

"What the hell'd you pull, stud? Got the boss lady hot for you?"

"Maybe. You'd have to ask her," Shelter said slowly setting himself, his own hand dropping slowly toward his holster to poise there.

"Gant was listening," Foley said. "He heard you tell the boss I ain't shit."

"She asked me, I told her. It was 'bout what she had figured anyway," Morgan said as Dent and Bishop slowly eased out of the way. The kid, Carl Pierce, seemed to want some of Foley but Morgan, glancing at him, shook his head. "We can work together, Foley, the only thing is you've got to realize who's boss now."

"You."

"That's right."

"Fuck you, boss!" Foley said and both hands flashed down toward his holstered guns. Morgan's came up first. The walnut-handled worn Colt he carried wasn't as pretty as Foley's twin revolvers, but it pumped lead just as well and Shelter's first bullet ripped through Foley's jaw, tearing the lower half of his face away as Foley's twin

Colts fired into the earth, lifting him onto his toes.

The outlaw staggered back, still trying to bring his guns to bear, but he didn't have the strength to lift his iron. Morgan's shot had cut the fiber out of him.

"You . . ." Foley said through the blood that flooded his mouth, and as he took another wobbly step back he dropped his guns, flopping onto his face to lie in the dust.

From across the camp men came running, Gant at their head. He looked at Foley and then at Shelter's smoking Colt. "I thought he was good," Gant growled.

"He was," Morgan said quietly.

Gant wanted to say something else to Morgan, but he didn't. To the gunmen gathered behind him, he said, "Bury him." Then, "Boys, this is the new top dog. His name's Martin. What he says goes." He looked at Morgan. "The boss says not to forget about dinner," Gant said as if it hurt him. "I'll have someone take your gear up to the main house."

Gant spun on a heel and stalked away. The outlaws put their weapons up and dragged Foley toward the pines. Dent and Bishop moved forward to shake Shell's hand.

"Thought you were bullshitting us, Martin. Things are looking better around here now."

"They'll get better yet," Morgan said, pausing as two raiders took his gear past. "There's big things going down and we're not settling for wages. Don't worry about a thing. We're saddle pals and I've got plans for you."

"Like what?" the kid, Carl Pierce, wanted to know.

"Big money," Shelter answered. "I'm watching out for you, believe me. All you boys have to do is stand with me—there's still people here who want to cut us out."

"Gant?"

"Yeah, he's one." Morgan lifted his eyes toward the

house. "Just remember this—it's cheap wages or a big payoff. We've got a handle on this, boys, I guarantee you. Hang in and we'll come out of this rich."

Then Morgan started off toward the house, hoping that he had touched the outlaws' lust for money and impressed them with his sudden power. They could be his only allies in the war to come—or they could be the ones to put that bullet in his back.

9.

Dinner was an intimate affair despite the size of the table in the huge dining room. The lady wore yellow. The dress was low cut and she kept leaning distractingly toward Morgan as she spoke. Morgan, in a dark blue suit and string tie, and wearing a fresh shave, tried to bring the conversation around to business, but Donna was having none of it.

"I don't talk business at the table. It's bad for the digestion," she said.

A Chinese in a white coat glided into the room from time to time, serving food on silver platters, refilling the wine glasses, and taking the empty plates away.

Morgan and the lady were the only diners. Apparently Gant was too low on the social scale to get himself invited. There was a fire burning brightly behind Shelter, warming his back, striking little points of bright light on the silver and crystal. The lady smelled of gardenias and she was beautiful, just beautiful.

Like a wildcat is beautiful. It wasn't hard to look at Donna, but knowing she had killed and ordered more killings ruthlessly took away some of Morgan's appetite for the roast goose and smoked pork the Chinese had served.

When there was nothing left but the pale wine, Donna said, "Would you like to see the rest of the house, Glen?"

"If you'd like to show it to me." Morgan folded his napkin and put it aside, helping the lady with her heavy chair.

"You've seen most everything down here," she said, letting her hand fall softly on Shelter's arm. "I'll show you the library. You might be surprised by it."

They climbed the stairs and entered one of the new rooms. Shell was struck again by the opulence of the place stuck away out here in the badlands of Dakota. Leather-bound books lined an entire wall. A desk with a leather top sat in one corner beneath two standing brass lamps. A bearskin, head down, was tacked to the wall.

"Like it?" she asked brightly. Her eyes were bright too, from the wine maybe.

"Very much."

"Come on. I'll show you something else you'll appreciate."

They walked down the corridor to a second room. Donna swung the door open and Shelter followed her into a white bedroom. All white. The walls, carpets, the canopy bed, the spread, the little satin pillows, the French dresser.

"This is my room." She sat on the bed. "Like it?"

"Beautiful," Morgan said.

Her eyes were brighter yet. She took off the silver bracelet she had been wearing and told him huskily, "Close the door, Morgan. Lock it."

She was out of her dress in seconds, and she wore nothing underneath. She walked to Shelter, her breasts bobbing hypnotically, and went to her knees to help him unbutton his trousers. When his erection sprang free she sighed with pleasure and held it to her cheek, caressing it as Morgan slipped from his shirt.

He kicked off his boots and carried her to the bed. Neither of them took the trouble to unmake it.

When the lady made love she was all teeth and nails, biting at Morgan, clawing his back as if releasing every emotion she had ever had, savage and violent.

"Now this way," she said, turning herself. "Now this way." She had no lack of energy. She bucked and pitched against Morgan, bringing herself to one violent climax after another. She fingered herself as Shelter jolted against her from behind, collapsing onto her face with another shuddering climax as Morgan lifted her higher and drove it in, finding his own sharp release as she moaned, her head rolling from side to side.

He lay on top of her for a long while and then rolled onto his back. The lady seemed to have had enough for the moment. She lay beside him, stroking his arm, one leg thrown up over his thigh.

"You're good," she murmured. "Very good. Are you as good a soldier?"

"Some say so," Morgan said, glancing down at the love-softened face, the babyish lips, the long-lashed eyes which were closed now. If you didn't know better you could almost take Donna for a human being.

"We'll find out tomorrow," she said, yawning. "I want you to get rid of some people for me. The Kennedy family. Gant will show you where their place is."

If she felt Shelter tense at the name she gave no sign of it. Her eyes remained closed and she cuddled closer to Morgan as the lamp burned low and night settled in.

Well, damn it all, he had invented the game. Now he

was going to have to prove up. And just how was he going to ride over to Boomer's place and burn it down? Shelter began to understand how thin a line he had drawn between life and death for himself. He worried over it for a long hour, but worrying wasn't going to solve it, and so he took the comfort of the woman's body in the night and dropped off to a troubled sleep.

In the morning Carlos was back.

Along with Foley, he had been one of the chief field officers for the raiders. He was a dark, scowling man with scars on his face and black eyes that measured Shelter carefully as Gant explained the new setup.

"Where do you come from, huh?" Carlos asked belligerently. "Who are you to come in here and take charge?"

Shelter wasn't about to be questioned. "Just remember I am the man in charge, and we'll get along."

Carlos fell into Spanish, cursing the tall man rapidly. Gant sipped at his whiskey and stared at his desk. Shelter couldn't blame them. They both had seen themselves as men on the way up, men reaching for a big piece of the pie, and now the lady had brought in a new general to run her war.

"You run into any army patrols?" Shelter asked Carlos.

"No. Not this time," he answered grudgingly. "It was a good trip. Some miners up along Little Horse Creek wouldn't take the message last time. They understood this time."

"Panther help you?" Shelter asked.

"He was there." Carlos shrugged. "We sent the Indians in. Then comes the *cavalry*. Us. The miners jump out from behind their barricades and wave to us. We rode

110

in and shot them all."

"You sure no one got away?"

"No one gets away when Carlos goes to work."

The voice from the doorway turned their heads. "Is everything settled?" Donna asked. She wore black slacks and a green shirt.

"Yeah, if this is the way it's going to be," Carlos answered.

"This is the way it's going to be. For now. If things don't work out we'll make some changes."

"All right, fair enough," Carlos said. His tone showed that it wasn't all right at all.

Donna told him, "Martin's making a little raid this morning, Carlos. I want you to go along with him."

"I just rode in," Carlos argued.

"I told you what I wanted!" she answered sharply.

"All right."

"Take some of the regular men along. Martin, take your new crew and see how they work out. Eight or ten men should be plenty."

"No uniforms?" Morgan asked.

"No, we've about used that gimmick up. Somebody's going to get wise. Besides, you shouldn't need an edge with just an old man and his daughter."

Outside, Shelter told Donna, "Carlos doesn't like me. You really think you ought to send him along?"

"He knows the back trails. You don't like company, Martin?"

"What sort?" he asked, stepping nearer to the lady. "Yours or his?"

Donna laughed. "We'll get along. Just do what you're told, right?"

"Sure. When's your brother riding in?" Shelter asked

casually, but the lady's face stiffened and he realized he had gone a step too far.

"I don't know. It doesn't concern you. You don't need him to do your job."

Then she walked back into the house, leaving Morgan to walk to the bunkhouse and collect Dent, Bishop, and Pierce. "Let's go, boys."

"What's up?" Dent asked.

"A little work."

"Good," Carl Pierce said. The kid swung his boots to the floor and sat up on his bunk.

Morgan looked around carefully. "Listen, you men watch yourselves, all right?"

Dent said, "We've been in a fight or two, Martin."

"That's not what I mean," Shelter answered. "There might be some trouble with our own people."

"What are you talking about?" Bishop growled.

"Just this—Foley talked us all down. A lot of the other boys who've been here longer don't want to cut the cake with us. They don't like me taking over as honcho. I had to fight to get you boys in on this. There's a character named Carlos who fancies himself as the big man. He has it in for me."

"A Mexican, huh?" Dent said, and Shelter encouraged him in whatever he might have thought he had against Mexicans.

"Right. You get the picture."

"We see how it is," Dent said. "Don't worry about it, Martin. We're in this together."

By the time they had collected their gear and weapons and gone out into the yard, Carlos had five of his men mounted and waiting. Dent looked at Carlos and then glanced at Shelter. Shell nodded in return.

112

Morgan had his pinto brought over, then he swung aboard and rode up beside Carlos.

"Ready now?" the raider asked caustically.

"Ready. Take the lead if you know where this place is."

Carlos looked at the three Kansas gunhawks. "Brought your own little army, did you?"

Shelter answered more loudly than he had to, "What's wrong with bringing along a few boys I know I can trust?"

"You don't trust me?" Carlos asked. Morgan didn't answer and Carlos shrugged. They started out of the camp then, and glancing back toward the house Shelter saw the little lady with the dark hair lift a hand in farewell.

By the time this day was done, Morgan thought, she wouldn't be so friendly.

They rode south through the Tangles toward Little Trace beyond. No one spoke much, Carlos least of all. He was tired and didn't like the idea of guiding the man who was going to replace him.

The land began to grow familiar. They passed the bluffs where Ruiz had been holed up and then the honeycomb caves.

"Let's head up to high ground at the first chance," Shelter said.

"Yeah, why?"

"I want to have a look around, that's why. This is a hell of a place to get trapped."

Carlos was arguing just for the sake of argument. He had been around long enough to know that the Tangles was no place to come upon an army patrol. At first opportunity they rode up out of the canyon and onto the

113

piney bluff where Cooney's cabin was, where Shelter and Boomer had spent the night not long ago, although it seemed a long, long time back.

In half an hour they were on the cliffs above Little Trace itself, where Morgan had seen the tracks of the watchers. "How far?" he asked Carlos as they wound through the trees.

"Not long now. You'll see it half a mile or so ahead, down on the flats."

"I'm going to go ahead and have a look," Shelter said.

"Alone?"

"That's right. Swing down and let the horses rest."

Carlos didn't like that, but he didn't argue. He just glared at Shelter with black, angry eyes. Morgan held up his pinto until Dent and the others caught up.

"I'm going ahead to look the place over. Watch yourselves, Dent."

"Don't worry about that."

"All right. It's just that I'd hate to have Carlos go back and report that we were all unfortunately killed on this job. Get me?"

"I got you," Dent said quietly, lifting his eyes to the Mexican.

Shelter turned his horse toward the deeper woods and rode higher up yet, pausing twice to make sure he wasn't being followed. Returning to the edge of the cliffs he could see the Kennedy cabin, smoke rising from its stone chimney. Maybe Boomer making supper for her father. He couldn't see the old man in his fields, so maybe that was a good guess.

Then he saw what he needed.

A column of soldiers heading away from the ranch. Maybe a mile off. Shooting would bring them back at the

114

gallop. But it had to be soon, before they were out of earshot.

Swinging the pinto, Morgan unholstered his Colt and held it beside his leg as he rode back.

It didn't matter who was first. The whole damn bunch of them were killers, cold-blooded murderers in it for the money. It just gave Shelter some satisfaction that it was Carlos, riding alone, who he met.

"Well, what the fuck you gonna do?" Carlos demanded.

For an answer Morgan brought the Colt up and blew the outlaw leader off his horse with a .44 slug through his heart. Carlos's horse reared up and started away at a dead run. As an afterthought Shelter fired another round into the air.

Then he swung down from his pinto, hied it away with a slap on the flank, and set up behind a huge pine with his Winchester.

Bishop, followed by Carl Pierce, came charging into the woods. Morgan stepped out and flagged them down.

"What happened?" Pierce asked breathlessly. His pale face was drawn tight. His well-notched Colt was in his hand.

"Bastard tried to ambush me. He missed. I didn't."

Dent's horse came pounding toward them, and behind him were Carlos's men, guns drawn.

"The game's up," Dent shouted. He turned his horse and opened up with his rifle, sending a man spilling from his horse to be dragged by the stirrup. A bullet tagged Bishop on the thigh, and as he fired back in a rage a second plowed into his skull, making a mask of blood of his face.

Dent took a second raider down and then dove for

115

cover. Shelter pumped four rounds through his Winchester, sending another raider to hell.

Pierce had guts. He waited in the raiders' line of fire, emptying his pistol into the onrushing band. He tagged one man and then thought better of his position. He spurred his horse toward cover but a raider slug caught the pony in the haunch, taking it down. Pierce was spilled into the underbrush.

Shelter took down the last raider and then turned, smiling toward Dent. "Sorry," he said, and Dent's eyes opened wide. He backed away and then tried a snap shot at Shelter which missed and knocked a dozen pine cones from a tree. Shell didn't miss. His bullet ripped through Dent's body and the killer fell forward on his face to lie still.

It was over, suddenly over. Nothing but a complaining jay moved in the woods. Shelter snatched up the reins to the pinto and heeled it out of there.

Below, he could see the column of blue-clad soldiers riding hard toward the Kennedy place. He made his way down the bluff and rode to join them.

It was Ball's patrol. They came into the yard of the ranch house with dust swirling, rifles at the ready, Ball with his saber drawn. In the doorway, also armed, were Kennedy and Boomer.

"Lieutenant Ball—" Shelter began. That was as far as he got.

"You are under arrest!" Ball shouted from the back of his bay horse.

"You can't arrest me," Shelter answered.

"The hell I can't. You wouldn't know it, but this territory has been placed under martial law. Sergeant Hicks! Arrest this man."

"If you'll let me explain . . ."

"Hicks!"

"Damn it, Ball, you're going to screw everything up."

Ball had swung down to walk to the doorway and talk to Kennedy. Shelter, taken from his horse and disarmed, listened as Boomer stared. "What happened, Kennedy?"

"Damned if I know. I heard shots, just like you."

"What was it, Morgan?" Ball demanded, spinning to face Shelter.

What was the point in telling him? What would Ball do? Ride out to the camp and get his patrol slaughtered, arrest Shell on a murder charge? No matter what he did he would ruin Shelter's "in" with the gang—assuming he still had one after today.

There was still an army connection to the raiders, too. Was it Ball who supplied uniforms to them? There was no telling about any of that, but there were too many negative points to be ignored. Shelter just clammed up, shutting his mouth.

Ball stepped to him and backhanded Morgan across the face. Blood seeped from Shelter's lips. "Damn you," he panted, "I asked you a question, Morgan."

"I don't have an answer for you."

"You can't get away with that!" Boomer Kennedy shouted. Ball glanced at her disparagingly. Morgan thought the officer was going to hit him again just to show her he could damn well do it if he wanted to, but Sergeant Hicks turned him away before Ball could decide.

"Come on," Hicks said.

"Is he crazy?" Morgan asked, spitting out the blood.

Hicks didn't answer except to move his eyes. Shelter and his horse were led to one side while Ball finished

117

talking with Kennedy. Boomer, in a fury, stood with her hands on hips alternately glaring at Ball and looking to Shelter.

When Ball strode back he snapped at Hicks, "Is that man a prisoner, Sergeant?"

Hicks stammered, "Of course . . . you said to take him prisoner, sir."

"Then damn it, treat him like a prisoner. Tie his hands behind him."

Ball swung aboard his own horse and sat looking northward, apparently still wondering what had happened. Hicks tied Shelter's hands—not too tightly, but tight enough to do the job. "I guess I'm lucky he didn't bring manacles along," Morgan muttered.

"Look, Morgan, I expect the lieutenant is wrong. I dunno. I know this though; he's got the authority to have you shot if he decided, though he'd be explaining a long time. I wouldn't step on his toes anymore if I were you. Odds are the captain will see things different."

"Are we going back to the post?"

"Yeah. Three days out is enough."

Morgan couldn't afford that. He couldn't go back to Fort Randall and lose all chance of breaking up the raiders. That meant he was going to have to try an escape at the first opportunity.

And that would give Ball just the excuse he wanted to have Morgan shot if he failed.

10.

They rode south and east, away from the Tangles. Shelter sat grimly among the columns of soldiers. With each mile he was getting farther from where he wanted to be.

There didn't seem to be much hope of getting away riding like this. Maybe by nightfall, but then they would be so far from the Tangles that they could run him down before he reached it.

He rode on in silence, glowering. Ball's stiff narrow back was a target for visual daggers. There was no satisfaction at all in knowing that he could have Ball's ass back at Randall. He didn't have any interest in getting even. He wanted to stop the raiders.

Ball's hand suddenly shot up and the column halted raggedly. It took Morgan a long minute to see what was happening, and then he made out the incoming rider.

He was a soldier, clinging to his horse uncertainly, wobbling in the saddle, and it became clear why in another minute. Blood smeared a torn tunic. There was a broken arrow sticking out of his left side.

Hicks said, "Damn it! It's Lieutenant Hodges."

119

The big-shouldered former enlisted man made it to the head of the column, saluted raggedly, and fell from his horse.

Morgan swung down and went foward—no one stopped him. He was in time to hear Harry Hodges murmur, "Panther . . . wiped us out to the man . . . water, for God's sake, Ball!"

He never got his water. He was dead before a canteen could be handed down. Ball rose, wiping his hands on his trousers, staring off to the south. There was confusion on his face. What did he do now? Pursue Panther, who obviously had them outnumbered if he had wiped out Hodges's patrol? He had little hope of catching him if he wanted to—and did he want to?

There was *still* the army connection.

Hodges had found a way to clear his name of suspicion. Was that the only way any of them could prove they were innocent?

Ball finally gave an order. "Bury him. We can't take him all the way back." He glanced at Morgan as if he didn't see him. Hicks had taken Shelter's arm, now he turned him back toward the pinto.

The soldiers swung down and waited, rifles ready as the detail planted Harry Hodges in the prairie earth. "If he spots us," Hicks said, "we'll get the same."

"A rider ought to be sent to Randall. Give him three horses. Get Captain Shirke out here now, with two full companies. You'll never get closer to Panther."

"That the way you'd do it, Morgan?" Hicks asked.

"Yes. Trail Panther cautiously, wait until Shirke arrived to make a war of it."

"That's the way I'd do it too," Hicks said quietly,

120

looking at Ball, who seemed to waver, leaning one way and then the other as if the prairie wind was moving him.

They weren't going to do that. They were going to get the hell out of there. In fact Ball took the patrol back toward the north, which suited Shelter. They were angling away from the local ranches, however; apparently there was going to be no attempt to warn the settlers. Maybe that was a waste of time anyway; everyone along the Little Trace knew that Panther was there.

Ball didn't strike Shelter as frightened, simply unsure. Had something gone wrong? Morgan was still dwelling on the fact that someone at Fort Randall was involved in this. Star Dan. PFC Lasky. The uniforms. The army's peculiar inability to find the raiders' camp.

That at least would be rectified when Shelter got back.

Of course, by then it would very likely be too late. Too late for the Kennedys and other Trace settlers.

They were into timber now and Shelter was watchful, waiting for a chance to make his break. It came as they dipped through a gulley, the column temporarily strung out single-file. Ball was already over the crest, the soldier behind Shelter was lagging.

He heeled the pony sharply and the pinto broke for the trees. The horse responded well to knee pressure and Morgan was riding as swiftly as if he had reins in his hands. Behind him was a shout and then a single shot. Horses were pursuing hard, but already Morgan thought he had them beat. Would Ball spend much time looking for him now? Shelter thought not.

He ducked a low limb and guided the horse back down into the gulley, doubling back a few hundred yards before he halted the pinto. He could hear confused searching in the woods. When he could hear nothing he slid from the pinto's back, stepped over his bound wrists, brought them up before him, and began working at the knot with his teeth.

It took five minutes but he finally shook the tie loose, swung aboard the pinto again, and beelined it north.

There was no telling what he was riding into. Donna would be furious. Morgan was unarmed and alone, truly alone now that Dent and his sidekicks were gone. He would have to rely on his influence with Donna to walk through this one.

It wasn't much to pin a hope of survival on.

It was late afternoon when he trailed into the outlaw camp, drawing dark looks from the men there. They looked up the trail behind him expectantly, but there was no one else coming. Shelter rode right up to the main house. There was no way of putting it off.

He looped the pinto's reins loosely around the hitching rail and walked up into the house.

He saw Donna immediately and took the offensive. "God damn it all! What'd you do, lady? Set me up?"

She was angry and shocked and concerned at once. "What are you talking about, Martin, what's happened?"

"I'll tell you in a minute. Have you got a goddamned drink?"

"Yes, certainly." She led the way into the dining room, Morgan stumping after her. He looked just bad enough, he thought. He was trail dusty and there was dried blood on his face and shirt from Ball's blow.

She poured him a shot of whiskey and he tossed it down, asking for another one. When he had poured that one down too she asked, "What happened?"

"Somebody screwed it up good. Panther hit an army patrol and they ran. They ran right into us. The army opened up. What was the Indian doing in the same area? Christ, the army was looking for anything that moved."

"He was supposed to be south . . . Hello, Gant."

Shelter turned to see the dark-eyed foreman. He walked slowly to Shelter, standing in front of him for a long minute without saying a word.

"The boys say you're the only one that rode in."

"That's right. Dead men don't ride," Morgan said coldly.

"They ran into an army patrol. They'd already been in a skirmish with Panther and were looking for raiders," Donna said.

"Good story," Gant said slowly. Shelter took a step toward the man, but Gant didn't back away.

"What're you saying, Gant?"

"Nothin'. Just seems funny you run into a patrol and only the new general gets back."

"Hell," Morgan said acidly. "I made it up. I ambushed our people myself. Shot 'em all down. Man, I'm quick with a gun."

"Maybe you had help. Your pals, for instance."

"Yeah, ride on out there and look. My pals are as dead as anyone else. I don't like this line of talk, Gant. I'm pissed. I lost my friends, I lost part of Donna's army."

"Yeah. Poor guy," Gant said despite Donna's look of protest. "How'd you get away, Martin?"

"The army took me prisoner. I waited until I got the chance and busted free."

"Sure."

"I'm lying again. Look, Gant," he said, holding out his wrists for both of them to see. "I even tied myself up. Now that takes more talent than gunning down ten men all by myself. I'm a whiz!"

Even Gant began to believe the tale. Nobody tied himself up. Donna said quickly, "Look, it doesn't matter for now. We lost some soldiers. We'll buy some more."

"And send them out again with Martin?"

"If I decide to, Gant. You're stepping over the line."

"Sorry, Mizz Drake." He didn't look a bit sorry.

"If you don't mind, I'm going to get some sleep," Morgan said. He and Gant continued to lock eyes. The man knew something, or maybe he just smelled it.

"Sure," Donna said with a worried smile. What she was worried about Morgan couldn't be sure. His health, or the possibility that he was something other than he was pretending to be.

He stumped upstairs to bed, locking the door behind him. Then he went to stand at the window and look out over the camp and the Tangles beyond.

"You'd better figure something out, Shelter," he told himself. "There isn't much time."

He couldn't pull another stunt like he had that morning. What could he do to cripple the raiders? Very little. And there was still Panther.

It was vital that he find out *who* was behind this now. He knew why but that wasn't enough. The head of the organization had to be found and then cut off. As Donna said, they could always hire more warriors. Fighting men came cheap.

He stretched out on the bed for a time, but he didn't even come close to falling asleep. He stared at the ceiling feeling like a prisoner awaiting the death penalty.

An hour or so later, hearing riders coming in, he swung his feet to the floor and walked to the window. Four men coming in hard, all of them wearing dark rain slickers. It had started to sprinkle outside already and looked like it was building to a good hard rain. Morgan saw Donna step out of the house and hug one of the new arrivals. He couldn't see his face. They hurried into the house while the other three took care of the horses.

The boss had just arrived.

Donna's brother ready to take charge personally perhaps. Ready to measure the new general with eyes less adoring than Donna's. The only thing Morgan could do was to bluff it out now. So far his game had worked, so far his luck had held. But he needed it to hold a little longer, long enough for him to identify the ringleader and then take off at the first opportunity.

It was Donna who knocked on his door a little while later. She was smiling as she came in and kissed his cheek. "Come on over to the library, Glen. There's someone I want you to meet."

"Oh?" Shelter tried to look surprised.

"My brother's just ridden in. We're getting ready for the big push. We'll join up with Panther and make one hard sweep through the valley."

"And then?"

"And then we pull out, letting the army know where they can find the Cheyenne. When that's been mopped up, we come back."

"Will it work?"

125

"It'll work," she said as Shelter walked out the door with her on his arm. "We have people inside the fort. People whose word won't be doubted as to what happened."

Morgan still couldn't figure out just who that was, but as they stepped into the library and the man at the bar turned toward them, he had it figured.

"Kill him," Lieutenant Doran said.

The blond kid Shelter remembered from the fort had just been a baby, soft, probably not needing a shave every day. Now as he sipped at his drink his face was a lot older, his eyes a lot crueler.

Gant had been behind the door, and he slipped Shell's Colt from his holster with a grin of triumph. Shelter heard his own gun being cocked behind him as Donna looked around in confusion.

"Not here, you idiot," Doran said to Gant.

"All right," Gant said. Then, just to get a little satisfaction out of things, he kicked Morgan hard behind the knee, folding his leg up, flooding Shell's body with pain. Shelter went to the floor and lay there.

"What is this!" Donna was screaming. "Why did you do that."

Doran had peeled off his slicker to reveal his army uniform underneath. "Don't you know who this is?"

"He's Glenn Martin . . ." Donna said helplessly.

"No, he's not. Shelter Morgan. Captain Shirke's chief scout—if he's not something a little more than that. Ball couldn't get him thrown off post. Shirke screwed up once and called him 'sir.' I thought it was just a mistake or a courtesy, but it wasn't. Whoever he is—and I really don't want to take the trouble to find out—he's working

126

for the army."

"You bastard!" Donna screamed. "You rotten bastard!"

She flung herself at Morgan, yanking at his hair, clawing at his face, trying to throw a knee. Doran, laughing, dragged her off as she continued to curse Shelter, to kick at him.

"What happened, Sister? Did your lover betray you?"

"Give me a gun! I'll kill him myself."

"That wouldn't be ladylike, would it? Besides, he might manage to charm you out of it. Gant will take care of that matter."

Donna's lip was curled back. She was a wild thing, killing mad. Doran continued to smile, but his smile was no more appealing than her twisted anger.

"Mind telling me about it now?" Shelter said, rising to lean a bracing hand against a red velvet chair. Doran had no reason to talk, but people who think they've done something really clever need to talk about it.

"Why not?" Doran replied. "You know almost all of it by now anyway, I imagine."

"How'd you get the idea? How'd you pull it off?"

"That was the simplest part," Doran said, leaning back against the desk, drink in hand. "I was the surveyor in charge of mapping the territory—you look a little surprised, Morgan. It's true. A friend of mine, Jack Yawky, and myself were hired to do the work. It wasn't much of a job—the renegades were everywhere. Jack and I missed a small piece of land and had to do the job over. We talked about that—what if a lot of land was overlooked. Who would own that land? Hell, no one would settle out here for years and years. No one had seen the land. What was down on paper was the reality.

"Jack was a reader. He recalled a tale of a man who bought a South Sea island for a few beads. It should have belonged to Spain, but the cartographers had left it off. Since it didn't exist it didn't belong to anyone until this man showed up.

"His claim was held up in court."

"You needed more than a few beads to make your plan work."

"That's right. There was still the Indians, still the army. And then these settlers. I started back east to work on things."

"With Yawky?"

Doran shook his head slightly. "Poor Jack didn't make it out of Dakota."

"I didn't figure he did," Shell said.

"I needed to be out here to manipulate things. I needed to come and go unsuspected. Then I got the idea of taking an army commission. It didn't take a lot of string-pulling to get me out to Fort Randall. They're always short of officers out here, and you'd be surprised how few volunteer for Dakota duty. After four weeks as a commissioned officer, I was right where I needed to be with the means to finish things up."

"And none of this bothers you?" Morgan asked. Doran just looked at him as if he had asked the question in a strange language.

"It's all very simple, really. Use the Indians to eliminate the settlers and later the army to eliminate the Indians. Fortunately I can put an army patrol where I want it while the renegades make their raids, then put the Indians where I want them when the army strikes back."

"The army uniforms?"

128

"Just a little confusion thrown in. I had Sergeant Stoner requisition those—he was well paid. I didn't want the people trusting even the army too much."

"Star Dan?"

"Star Dan saw too much. Lasky killed him for me."

"Then you killed Lasky."

"Some of Panther's men did it, actually. Around the post there was too much suspicion that the renegades weren't responsible for everything. Some of my people were a little too queasy about mutilations and scalping."

"That must have been disappointing to you," Morgan said icily. The bastard was one of the coldest little killers Shelter had run up against. Cunning, he had no idea what a conscience might be. His sister was as bad. Morgan wondered what kind of upbringing the two of them had had.

"And Ball?" Shelter asked.

"Ball! That stiff-necked fool? He's no part of this."

"You got Hodges, didn't you?"

"Panther." The kid shrugged. "I just told him where Hodges could be found. That should stir Shirke up . . . It's really necessary that we finish with the settlers right now. Then the army can finish it for me." Doran was watching Shelter. "What's the matter? Hard to believe I could have pulled this all off, that it is going to work?"

"It's not that. I was wondering whether or not I was going to puke," Shelter answered.

Doran's smile was washed away by an expression as twisted and violent as his sister's. He started toward Morgan, halted, and told Gant, "Get him out of here. Kill him."

Then Shelter was spun around and Gant, looking at him over the Colt, gestured toward the door. Outside it

129

was raining hard, the wind shaking the trees with cold hands.

Gant took him up into the trees until they had reached a small clearing among the big pines. "That's far enough," the outlaw said.

Shelter turned, looking at the small mounds that filled the clearing. He wasn't going to be the first, it seemed. But he was going to be the one Gant enjoyed the most.

11.

"This all your work?" Shelter asked, nodding at the graves around him. Anything to make life last a minute longer. Talk. Feel the rain on your face, the cold wind. It was even good to feel his body shivering with the cold, good to see Gant's little eyes sparkle with hatred. It was life, and Morgan wasn't ready to give up his own yet.

"Not all mine. A few."

"Men who got out of line?"

"Something like that. It doesn't matter. They're gone and you will be too in a minute."

Gant didn't want to finish it too quickly either. He was standing there savoring the moment, his gun held out before him.

He's not going to do it, Shelter thought. It wasn't a rational thought, but it flitted through his mind just before Gant lifted his pistol and the gunshot rang harshly through Morgan's skull.

Shell reflexively threw himself to one side, and it was from there that he looked back, watching Gant sway on his feet, open his mouth which flooded with hot blood, and then fall.

Morgan's eyes narrowed. He lay frozen for a second

before lifting himself to his feet. He took Gant's gun and still didn't figure what had happened. The wind lifted his dark hair. His shirt was plastered to him with rain.

Boomer came slowly from the trees, rifle under her arm, hat pulled low, wearing a long buffalo coat. "I swear, Morgan, you just don't seem to be able to take care of yourself."

"We'd better get out of here," Morgan said.

"Yeah. That's what took me a minute. I was watching down the hill to see if any of 'em came up after the shot, but they must figure it was Gant giving it to you, Shell."

"You're crazy for coming out here," Shelter said. He was smiling as he pulled her against him.

"Yeah, maybe. I just didn't know what was going to happen to you when the soldiers took you off. I been following along pretty much since then."

Shelter pulled her to him and kissed her mouth. It tasted sweet; her lips moved against his provocatively, hungrily. Then she stepped back sharply.

"You know you got scratch marks on your face?"

"I had a little tussle back there."

"Yeah?" Her eyes narrowed with suspicion. "I never seen a man with claws like that, nor one that would fight by scratching at another man's face."

"I didn't say a man did it," Shelter growled. "Let's get out of this clearing." But Boomer was still rooted.

"A woman? She must've been awful mad, Morgan. Just what was going on down there, anyway?"

"Ugly old outlaw woman wanted me to do nasty things to her and I wouldn't."

"Yeah? I'll bet."

"It doesn't matter. Where's your horse."

"Upslope," she answered, but she was still staring at

132

those scratch marks.

"Then, come on. If Gant doesn't go back down there, someone will come looking."

"Yeah." Boomer shouldered her rifle and tramped off upslope like a little soldier in that big buffalo coat. Her horse was hitched to a broken pine behind a stand of boulders. "We'll have to go double, looks like," Boomer said. "You get up behind and try to find something to hold onto."

"Sounds like fun, but I'm not going."

"You're what!"

"I'm staying behind here for a while."

"Quit joking, Shell!"

"I'm not joking."

"Then you're insane." She pointed downslope. "You came within about a second and a half of getting yourself blowed away down there. Now you're going to go back and give them a second chance?"

"After a while. After dark."

"But why!"

"Because they'll never expect it. Because they deserve it. Because that's what I'm being paid to do."

"What about me!" Boomer wailed.

"What are you going to pay me to do?"

"You know that's not what I meant."

Shell grinned. "Don't worry about it. I'm going to stay put until dark. Then do a little damage."

"Shit! Why do I bother keeping you alive? You just go right out and try to commit suicide again."

"Ride, Boomer." There was someone coming now. Shelter could see two men walking toward the trees across the camp of the outlaw yard.

"All right, damn you, Morgan!" Then she softened.

133

"If you want to find me, look at Cooney's. That's about as far as I can make it by nightfall anyway."

Then she climbed aboard and swung her horse away. Morgan watched her ride up and over the crest. Then he began to move himself. He moved along the slope, slanting downward toward a concealed pile of boulders and broken limbs he had seen to the north.

He heard a shout behind him, but glancing back could see nothing. They'd found Gant's body.

Shelter clambered up onto the rocks, found a little niche where he was out of the brunt of the wind and could see back down the trail as well, and settled in to wait.

As he had told Boomer, it didn't seem likely that anyone would think he had stayed around after killing Gant. They might try pursuing him, but in the Tangles, in the darkness of the day with the rain washing away any tracks, they would know they weren't going to find an elephant out there let alone a running man.

It was cold, damned cold. Shelter's teeth chattered. He hugged himself, his knees drawn up, and sat staring out through the rain toward the outlaw camp.

He couldn't forget the superior smirk on Doran's face, the twisted, half-mad expression on Donna's. They didn't give a damn how many people got killed, white, red, or any other. Only one thing in life mattered—their profit.

Morgan was determined they weren't going to profit from this.

He was soaked through, but his Colt was dry. He would endure. Endure for long enough to use it.

The rain started to break up about sundown. The clouds, woven together by the mesh of rain, now tore apart in ragged remnants of a storm. The sunset was deep red and piercingly brilliant gold. The Tangles, long dark and brooding, were colored eerily by it.

No one had ridden into the camp, no one had ridden out. If they were going to make their big push, Morgan had expected more activity. No search party had gone looking for him, so he guessed Doran had chalked it up to experience—next time maybe he would just let Gant stain his carpet. Morgan didn't mean for there to be a next time for anyone.

The stars began to blink on one by one and he stretched stiffly. It was still a long wait, a long cold wait, before he dared to go down into an armed camp. He looked to the east thinking of Boomer. He didn't much like the idea of her being in Cooney's cabin, but maybe she was safer there than she would have been at the home ranch in the way of Doran's raiders.

Morgan shifted again. His leg was going to sleep. His knee made a cracking sound as he moved.

Ball—maybe he owed Ball an apology, but Shelter didn't think so. He wasn't a renegade at all, just pigheaded, a strutting little man— Something moved down below and Shelter shifted his head, squinting downward. It was hard to tell, but it looked like four men were wheeling a wagon from the barn across the yard. They were partly screened by oaks and it was awfully dim.

Why the wagon? Shelter couldn't figure it, so he let it go. Now, under the cover of darkness, riders began to filter into the camp from out of the Tangles, reinforcements for the morning push. Other riders left, maybe to take up positions, or to run messages to Panther.

Maybe to search for the man who was sitting above

them with a cold hatred growing in him. These were men who made war not on an opposing army but on women and kids and hard-working men. What the Indians and hard weather, rocky soil, stumps, locusts, and drought hadn't been able to do, these men meant to do by force of arms.

Well, it wasn't going to happen that way. Those people weren't going to be driven off and they weren't going to be killed.

Big talk for a man alone. Shelter's mouth tightened. He sat watching, waiting.

He let the hours creep by, the stars slowly arc over, but still there were men working in the yard when he decided he had to go on down or forget it. The lights were off in the big house. There was a single light in the bunkhouse. Otherwise the dark night absorbed all illumination.

But not at the barn. Damn it, that bothered Shell.

He rose carefully, feeling fragile and frozen, as if by moving too quickly he could snap something off. He could hardly walk at first, from the stiffness and from the cold that had invaded his body and caused his legs to tremble violently.

After a little walking he felt better, almost alive. He made his way cautiously downslope although he had no real fear of being seen. He kept to the trees and circled toward the back of the barn, seeing the torches burning brightly, hearing an occasional muttered complaint.

Easing up behind stacked hay, he was able to look all the way through the double doors of the old barn to where firelit raiders worked.

"I still don't like the idea of giving guns to an Indian, whether he's supposed to be on our side or not."

"Nobody asked you, Jacobs . . ." That voice was

136

vaguely familiar, but Shell couldn't make out the faces of the men who moved around the wagon.

They were hoisting a crate onto the wagon which was already pretty well loaded, judging by how high up they had to hand the crate. Horses were already hitched to the wagon. One shifted its feet and blew impatiently.

Shelter moved a little nearer, easing his way through the thick shadows to the back of the barn.

"What's left?"

"Two small ammunition boxes and that's it."

The man who had been complaining said, "I hope none of them bullets has my name on it."

"You're getting paid enough to risk it."

"Just keep thinking how I'd feel knowing that we gave them the guns to finish us."

There was a clunking sound, another curse, and the sigh of wagon springs as a third man leaped down from the wagon, closed the canvas top, and stood wiping his forehead.

"We could've used some help on that."

"It's done now. Besides, you know the boss. He don't want one man to know what the other's doing."

"When's it going out?"

"Tonight. Harry and I are taking it." A silence followed that and then the same man added, "Yeah, swell job, ain't it. I'm getting a nice bonus, but still, I don't like it."

"Me I'm gonna have a dab of whiskey and go to sleep. You boys watch yourselves."

"Wait a minute." This one took the lantern from the other one and blew it out. "It's too damned cold. Harry? One drink for the road?"

Harry looked off toward the big house and shrugged.

137

The three men walked away into the darkness and Shelter moved into the barn. Looking around, he found a pitchfork and began strewing straw across the floor of the barn, working like a madman in the darkness.

He spent five hard minutes doing that and then moved to the team, silently dropping the traces. He led the team forward and the tongue fell, making too much noise by far.

The lantern was hung on a nail on the wall, and there was a box of matches resting on the nailkeg below it. Looking out the door once Shelter backed in again, yanked the lantern, and unscrewed the filler cap. He was spreading this over the straw when the outlaw, shotgun leveled, appeared at the back doors.

"What the hell's going on here?" he demanded, peering into the darkness, trying to make out Morgan's face. "Who put the lamp out?"

"Harry and them went to collect their gear. They're moving out in five minutes."

"All loaded?" There was puzzlement and caution still in the guard's voice. He inched forward and then he smelled it. "What the hell . . . ! What are you spreading there?"

Morgan dove to one side, the lamp chimney smashing against the floor. The shotgun roared in the night as Shell rolled behind a partition between stalls.

Shelter's Colt barked a harsh answer and the gunman was lifted to his toes, the second barrel discharging into the ground. Morgan raced toward the team. Behind him there were running footsteps coming, many of them.

He struck three matches at once, slapped the off horse on the flank, and held on while the team took off for the back door. The matches arced into the night like tiny dying embers and brought the barn to sudden fiery life.

Shelter's horses bumped over the dead outlaw's body and swung into the oaks behind the barn. Already he could feel the heat of it, see red and golden flames curling into the sky as smoke drifted heavily through the night.

He saw two men with wet blankets try to fight their way through the flames and then retreat. A shout went up and they all seemed to figure it at once.

Morgan leaped from the team and stood waiting, watching. When the fire hit the ammunition the barn quivered, seemed to lift from the ground, and then blew apart in a million fragments of flying lumber. Shell saw one raider blown backward nearly fifty feet. Another, his leg obviously broken, was afire as he crawled away, calling for help—but no one wanted to go any nearer to the barn. Another explosion racked the night. Now the lights were blazing in the big house and Morgan looked that way, his lips compressing and then drawing back in a very nasty grin.

Men with buckets were running in all directions, a lot of them in underwear and hats. Others staggered around, injured by flying debris, or lay on the ground moaning.

No one paid much attention to Morgan. He was outside of the firelight, in the deep shadows, and the place was an anthill where no one knew who was who or where they were going or cared.

Shelter moved to the back window of the house and peered in, seeing nothing. There was so much shouting, the flames so loud, that he didn't bother to muffle the blow as he struck the windowpane with the butt of his Colt, breaking it out.

He still had quite a few matches.

He touched flame to the corner of the curtain and it

went up like a moth's wings. Shell backed away, walked to the next window, and repeated the trick.

This time it didn't go so smoothly. The door suddenly opened and an outlaw burst into the room, pawing at his holstered gun. "Hey, you son of a bitch!" he yelled and Morgan shot him.

The bullet ripped its way through the raider's body, turning him, thudding into the wallpapered wall behind him. Morgan decided to do it right the next time. He recognized the room as Gant's office. He popped the window, opened the latch, slid it up, and stepped over the sill.

The hall door was closed, the room dark except for the reflected firelight. Morgan opened Gant's desk drawers and started throwing paper around the room . . .

By the time he stepped over the sill, the paper was soaked with kerosene from Gant's table lamp. When the match touched the fuel, it went up with all the vigor of the barn fire. Morgan walked away from the house slowly, then turned to watch his handiwork. He crouched down watching the flames begin to curl from the windows of the house, hearing someone with a shrieking voice yelling at the raiders to get over and put it out.

They weren't going to make it.

It was a cruel, violent, and deadly thing, that fire.

Funny. Morgan enjoyed it just fine. The warmth from it went right through his skin and muscle and glowed in his heart.

140

12.

The fires still blazed as Morgan made his way across the camp again. Once a man turned and looked at him in the darkness, puzzled, not quite remembering who Shelter was; but he hurried on toward the fire without incident.

It didn't take much to find a horse or to swing aboard and ride slowly out of the camp. Shelter rode briefly into the Tangles in case he was being followed, but there was no one on his backtrail. With the rain falling again—too late to save the burning buildings—Shelter turned the horse upland toward the mesa and Cooney's cabin, warming himself with thoughts of a long night spent with Boomer. In the morning he planned to ride to Fort Randall and explain the whole mess to Captain Shirke. The army, perhaps augmented by civilian volunteers, would find the raiders disorganized if they could get back out here in time.

The old cabin appeared from out of the trees, a dark and stodgy swaybacked thing among the huge pines. Shelter slowly circled the place before riding up to the back, unsaddling the borrowed horse, and tying it.

Then, with that warmth of anticipation still in him, his

loins stirring, he circled through the light rain to the front door.

The door stood open.

Frowning, Shelter unholstered his Colt. Boomer hadn't gone off and left the door open, nor would it be standing open if she were inside. He eased on through the doorway, gun held high besides his ear, his thumb on the hammer, finger on the cool, curved trigger.

He knew something was wrong immediately. The bed was spilled over on its side in the center of the room. Morgan's heartbeat picked up. The dark form in the corner of the room . . . it was only her bedroll.

He couldn't see much of anything. Finding the candle he struck a match to the wick and looked around a little better.

She hadn't gone easy. There was a bullet hole in the wall and a spot of fresh blood on the floor beneath it. The table had been slammed into the wall, the bedding strewn across the room.

Shelter found a casing from Boomer's rifle, but no other cartridges. He crouched looking at the bright brass of the casing for a minute and then flung it away. It rang off the stone fireplace and then the cabin was still again.

Still as death.

He didn't let himself think that way. If she was dead, why take her away from the cabin at all? No, she was alive, but she was a prisoner.

It was on the second inspection of the bloodstain that Shelter found something to chill his heart. A foot had been put down in the splotch of blood. Just the toe of the foot. Enough to see that it had been encased in an Indian moccasin.

Panther had her.

There was a roaring in Shelter's ears. He had seen editorials in the newspapers back East opining that the Indian wasn't the savage he was made out to be, that his warfare and treatment of prisoners was no worse than that of the whites. They knew everything, those men at their New York desks, except what an Indian captive looks like after they get through with him.

Or her.

Once, things might have been different, but the long war had changed everything. The savagery of the war had produced a savagery of heart where people were mutilated, battered, raped, burned alive.

But not Boomer—it wasn't going to happen to that little red-headed girl.

"Big talk," Morgan muttered. All right—amend that—it wasn't going to happen if Morgan could do anything to stop it.

Outside it was raining. He crouched close to the ground and searched until he found the six ponies' tracks lined out northward. Boomer's shod horse was traveling with them. He saddled up and started out through the dark and the rain. The tracking was incredibly slow. A dozen times in the first half hour Morgan swung down to search on foot for the tracks. They were still heading north and he could count on picking up their sign at intervals, but it wasn't easy.

And with each minute he was losing time on the renegade Cheyenne.

Dawn was a slow deep red flush against the banks of clouds. The rain still fell in fine slanting lines. The pines were heavy with water, the sun striking sparks against the droplets clinging to the needles. The scent was clean

143

and heavy in the air.

Shelter was well north of the Tangles now. The outlaw camp was far behind to the south and west. There seemed to still be a smoky smudge against the sky from the night of fires.

He didn't have to waste time casting back and forth for the renegade tracks now. They were cut deep in the rain-dampened earth, lining straight northward.

It didn't quite fit. The last time Shell had seen Panther he had been south, but then the renegade was a mobile force, striking here and there. This was the morning he was supposed to join with the outlaws in cleaning out the settlers for once and all. Yet Doran and his sister weren't going to be quite ready. Not for a little while.

There it was. Morgan felt exultation and cold fear at once. The renegade camp was dead ahead of him. Maybe fifty lodges, all of buffalo hides, grown shabby with use. Morgan could almost feel for Panther and his people. Once proud, riding the land to the sunset and beyond, they had taken a beating by a better-equipped army. Now they were beggars on the land, trying to set up an alliance with the outlaws to gain some of their lost land back.

Yeah, you could almost feel sorry for them if you hadn't seen Panther's work and didn't know the stories. Victory and defeat were the opposite poles of a warrior's life. Both occurred unpredictably. It was how a man handled them that counted. Morgan knew. He had been with a losing army for nearly five years, and if there had been some Southern fanatics who wouldn't let the war go and insisted on forming their own guerilla groups, Morgan had simply made a truce with his own feelings and walked away from that. Panther couldn't. He would fight no matter what price was exacted, both from his

144

people and from innocent whites.

He saw them then. Six Cheyenne renegades coming out of the trees, the wind shifting the feathers in their hair, moving the buckskin fringes on their shirts and leggings. They carried Winchester needle guns. One of them wore a Colt revolver on a holster around his neck.

There wasn't any point in trying to run, none in trying to fight.

Shelter lifted a hand and sat the horse as the renegades came nearer. They were all painted, all competent looking. But then you weren't going to run across a Cheyenne who wasn't war-tough and hard-country lean.

"Why come here to die?" the man in charge asked Morgan. He was tall for a Cheyenne, scarred, his nose once broken.

"Now Panther kills his friends?" Morgan asked.

The Indian just looked at Shelter, and Morgan knew he was being measured. If you weren't a warrior yourself you weren't going to get any respect at all from these men. Maybe the Indian saw a warrior in the icy blue eyes of the tall white; at any rate he was content to talk for a moment instead of killing Shelter out of hand, which is what Shell, his hand resting on his thigh near his revolver, expected them to try.

"Who is Panther's friend?" the Indian asked, turning his pony so that the rifle across his saddle had its muzzle toward Shelter.

"Me. Martin."

"I don't know you."

"You know the man who sent me," Shelter said, "or Panther does."

"What man?"

"Doran," Shelter replied and he saw the Indian's eyes

145

react to the name. It was a long bluff Shell was trying to run, but he had enough background on the raiders to have a chance at making it work. Besides, he had no choice unless he wanted to die and know that Boomer too was going to die, very slowly.

"Doran," the Indian repeated. "Maybe Panther knows him."

"Maybe he does."

"What has this to do with you?"

"Two things," Shelter said, trying a smile which went unanswered. "Doran sent me up to tell you that the rifles and ammunition were destroyed last night in a fire. The raid will have to be postponed."

The Indian's face darkened and he turned to speak rapidly in the Cheyenne tongue to the others. Morgan didn't get a word of it, but all of the renegades' eyes went colder yet.

"Is this a trick of Doran's?"

"Hell, you know it's not. What can Doran do without Panther by his side?"

The Indian didn't reply. There wasn't all that much trust between the two sides apparently. Maybe they could sense that Doran was setting them up, maybe they just had gone beyond trusting any whites.

"You said there were two things," the Indian reminded Shelter.

"Yeah, the other," he said casually, "is that some of your braves came and took my squaw last night. Guess they didn't know I was on your side. I want her back."

"Squaw?" Again the Indian turned his head and spoke to the others. One of them knew and said something in return. "Little small woman with flame hair?"

"That's her. I had to ride over to Doran's camp, and

146

when I got back she was gone."

"You know it was Cheyenne who did this?"

"I tracked them here," Shelter said and the Indian looked at Morgan with grudging admiration. That was no mean feat in the night and rain for any man.

"Panther will be unhappy about the rifles," the Indian said. "As for the squaw, I do not know. Ride down. We will be behind you."

"Yeah," Morgan said almost under his breath. They would be behind him all right, and their rifles would be ready.

They rode down into the grassy valley and renegade warriors emerged from their lodges to watch. There were no women, no children, no dogs. This was a fighting force. Beyond the village Morgan could see their spare horses, perhaps three to the man. A lot of them were army bays.

Morgan glanced back at his guide and had the way pointed with a rifle barrel. Panther's tipi stood on the edge of the camp. It had red magic signs painted on it, a ghost buffalo and a panther at its haunches.

Shelter rode up and swung down without being told to. No one had taken his guns yet, but that was remedied now. Someone stirred inside the lodge and then the flap was thrown back and Panther emerged.

He would have been recognized as a man of authority anywhere. Tall, broad at the shoulders with a hard, deeply muscled chest, he wore a bear claw necklace, leggings of elk hide, and a blanket thrown loosely over his shoulders. The eyes were as hard and black as obsidian, the mouth an expressionless slash across his bronze face. The face was lean, angular, with a nasty scar across one eye. The legend was that a white reservation teacher had

147

done it with the flat of a sword.

"So? Who is this?" Panther asked, speaking not to his men or to Shelter, but to the sky, as if Morgan had miraculously descended from another plane.

Shelter answered himself. "Glen Martin. I'm Doran's war leader now, Panther. We've had some trouble. Doran wanted me to tell you about it."

"Trouble?" Panther said tonelessly. His constant suspicion of whites lurked behind those black eyes and behind the single questioning word.

"Yes. We got hit last night. Someone burned down a few buildings. Your weapons were in the barn. They got destroyed by the fire. It'll take a little while to get new ones to you."

"Doran is lying to me," Panther said.

"I promise you he isn't," Morgan answered.

"And who are you to promise me!" Panther asked, coming nearer so that he was nearly in Shelter's face. "I do not know you. You may be anyone, you may tell me anything."

It wasn't going that well. Morgan had to play a card he didn't want to play. "Send someone down to have a look," he shrugged. "You'll find out I'm telling the truth."

"And you will stay here," Panther said. Morgan felt his belly tighten. Suppose someone did go down and talk to Doran. They would find out that the story of the fire was true, all right. And if they asked the wrong question they would also find out that Morgan wasn't quite what he was pretending to be.

Shelter looked into Panther's eyes. He could feel the other renegades pressing nearer, feel their body heat and smell them. An argument was out of the question.

148

Panther wasn't above killing an authentic Doran envoy, he knew. Kill the white and insist he had never shown up at all.

"All right. I'll wait. Meanwhile, Panther, there's a second matter to discuss."

"Yes?" Panther couldn't have shown less interest.

"Some of your people took my squaw. A red-headed girl."

"What do I care."

"*I* care," Morgan said. "And Doran will care. If you want those rifles and that chunk of land he's promised you, you'd best see that the squaw is returned unharmed."

"You threaten me," Panther said. The corner of his mouth turned up in a tiny, dirty smile.

"I tell you how it is," Shelter said, dropping his voice a little.

The renegade leader took a long time thinking it over as the cold wind blew across them. The guns and ammunition were all-important, and that was what Shelter had been banking on. Finally Panther turned away sharply.

"What do I care for a squaw?" He added something in his own tongue, and hands gripped Morgan by the arms, leading him away toward another tipi.

Shell was led across the camp and taken to another small tipi where a renegade stood watch outside, rifle cradled in his arms. Morgan was shoved inside none too gently. He managed to keep his footing and halt in the center of the lodge beside the fire ring. Boomer was in the corner, looking bedraggled but well.

"Morgan, you need a keeper," was the first thing she said.

149

He grinned and walked to her, sitting beside her to wrap his arm around her shoulders. "Still feisty, are you?"

"Feisty?" she shot back. "I'm downright pissed. What are you doing here!"

"I came after you."

"True love," she said mockingly. "Why, you idiot, now they've got the two of us to chop up."

"I told Panther that I was with the raiders."

"And he swallowed it?"

"Not exactly," Morgan had to admit, and Boomer shook her head in amazement.

"It's nice to know you really care about me, Shelter. I'll carry that thought to the grave—which doesn't seem to be very far off right now."

"It might work out. Panther's going to send someone down to the Tangles to make sure I was telling him the truth."

"The truth about what?" Boomer asked.

"About someone attacking the raiders' camp last night and destroying all the weapons his men were supposed to get."

"*Someone,* huh?" Boomer had to laugh. "You take the cake, Morgan, you surely do." More soberly she added, "We can't get away with it, you know."

"Maybe not. Popular as you are, though, I couldn't see you entertaining a hundred Cheyenne renegades."

"No." A chill ran through Boomer and she rested her head against Morgan's shoulder. "I've heard of it happening. It's as nasty a way of dying as there is. Used up. Thrown away."

"Yeah. Let's not talk about it. It won't happen."

"Guaranteed?" she asked, touching his cheek as she looked up into his eyes.

"Guaranteed." His smile wasn't very convincing. Boomer snorted.

"Save it for the schoolmarms."

"Yeah."

"What's your idea if the man Panther sends to the renegade camp comes back with the news that you're not who you claim?"

"I don't plan to be here by then," Shelter said. Boomer looked at him oddly. "I'm just trying to buy time. After dark we're getting out of here."

"Lovely," Boomer said, growing still more sarcastic. "What do we do, buy a ticket out or overpower the hundred warriors out there?"

"You worry too much," Morgan said.

"I take that answer to mean you don't know how to do it."

"Shut up," he growled.

"Uh-huh, that confirms it."

The lady was exactly right, but Morgan didn't admit it to her. He had no plan, all he knew was that he was going to try *something* before the Indians had a chance to decide what they wanted to do with Boomer.

With his pocketknife Shelter opened up a narrow slit in the tent and peered out at the goings-on. It was relatively quiet out there, with warriors walking back and forth or sitting together talking about old battles and those yet to come. There was a wrestling match farther across the camp that no one was paying any attention to.

They weren't situated too badly, Morgan decided, if they could get out of the tipi. The lodge was on the edge of

151

the camp, and beyond a little arroyo a hundred feet or so off the timber began.

Boomer was peering over his shoulder. Both of them drew back quickly, silently, as the legs of a guard appeared.

"No good," Boomer whispered.

"It's a chance. After dark."

"If we last that long."

Yeah, if they lasted that long. Boomer's head drooped a little and she dozed as time passed, but she came suddenly awake, for the first time since Shelter had known her actually looking frightened. She gripped his wrist so tightly that her nails bit into his flesh.

"Easy, girl," Morgan said quietly. "Scared?"

She slowly woke up all the way. Nodding, she said, "I was dreaming. They had gotten to the ranch. Dad was . . . didn't make it. Shelter, I should have stayed there to help him."

"One more rifle wouldn't have made any difference, kid."

"Maybe not, but still . . ."

"Besides," he reminded her, "it was only a dream. You know where the raiders are."

"Do we, do we, Shelter?"

It began to grow cool. Outside the sun was sinking slowly behind the pine ridge. "Listen, Boomer, if you get out of here you're going to have to try to make it to Fort Randall. Talk to Captain Shirke, no one else. Tell him what's going on out here."

"We'll go together, Shell."

"Yeah, if we can. But if we can't, do what I tell you. You know the Tangles and should be able to lose yourself out there. Too bad you don't have a horse, but maybe you can make it all the way back to your ranch. If you do, get your father out of there and head for Randall."

"All right, but—"

"No buts." He held her face, looking into her eyes. He kissed her lightly and then let his hands fall away.

"When do we try it?" Boomer asked with resignation.

"Right now."

13.

She watched with frightened eyes as Morgan walked to the tent flap. In Boomer's hand was Shell's pocketknife. She glanced at the slit he had cut in the tipi wall and then back at Morgan. In the near darkness she could swear he winked at her.

Morgan ducked out through the flap and Boomer ripped the buffalo hide open, slipping through it into the night.

The warrior turned on Shelter immediately. He was big and he had his rifle. Jabbing at Shelter he prodded him back toward the tipi.

"What's the matter? Just wanted some air," Morgan said.

The rifle prodded him again in the belly, and to make the point the renegade thumbed back the hammer of his rifle. Still Morgan didn't move. Instead he grinned, and the Indian's eyebrows drew together in puzzlement.

Five minutes. He had to give Boomer five minutes to reach the woods. She still might not make it, but at least she would have a chance. They weren't going to track her quickly in the dark, and if she made the Tangles, no one white or red was going to find her.

"You got tobacco?" Morgan said and he made an elaborate show of pretending to fill a pipe and smoke it while the befuddled guard watched the pantomime. "How about food?" He rubbed his belly. "We been in there all day."

Behind the renegade, Morgan could see other curious warriors drifting his way. There was the faintest red glow in the sky above the camp. Cookfires were glowing softly against the dark earth.

The renegade jabbed Shelter again, harder, and he had to step back into the tipi. The guard gave him still another shove, and then he was inside as well. He looked around in the darkness. Near one side of the tipi a dark figure lay against the ground. The Indian moved to it, poked it with his foot, and then let out a yell as he figured out it was nothing but a heap of blankets and Boomer was gone.

At the yell three warriors burst through into the tent and Morgan was dragged backward, his arms pinned, one of his captors slapping him hard across the mouth, spinning his head, flooding his mouth with hot, salty blood.

They half-carried him outside. Men on horseback were already riding out in different directions, one of them calling as he found Boomer's tracks.

Across the camp Panther waited outside his lodge. Fire from within lighted one profile. He didn't look happy at all. A hurried explanation made him look a lot less happy. Morgan was dragged inside the renegade leader's lodge and thrown against the floor.

Morgan sat up, spitting out dirt and blood. Panther's foot struck him in the chest and slammed him to the floor again, nearer the fire so that the flames scorched his cheek.

155

Panther was a dark menacing silhouette hovering over him. The renegade leader made a hissing sound between his teeth, an animal expression of disapproval and anger.

"You said you came as a friend," Panther said, his voice trembling with emotion.

"And you had me arrested," Shelter countered.

"The woman is gone."

"You said, 'What do I care for a woman?'"

"I do not want to play with words," Panther said. A renegade warrior slipped into the tipi, glanced at Morgan, and whispered something to his chief.

"It's not playing with words," Morgan said. "You promised the woman her freedom. I gave it to her."

"And how long do you think she will be free, *Morgan?*"

Shell felt his mouth go dry, the great veins at his temples begin to pound. "What did you say?"

But it was too late—the game was up. Doran ducked into the tent, wearing his second lieutenant's uniform and a mask of sheer hatred.

"You keep busy," Doran said. Then his booted foot swung out viciously and caught Morgan under the jaw. Shell was sent sprawling again. Pain flashed through his skull and the twinkling multicolored lights went on.

"I just came to explain about the guns," Morgan said, pushing himself away from the ground to sit grinning foolishly at Doran. And, Morgan was thinking, if he only had a gun in hand just then, he could end this war. One shot into the black heart of Doran, one into Panther's scowling face.

But he didn't have a gun, or a knife, or a pointed stick, and he could only take it as Doran kicked him again, this time in the ribs. Morgan heard a muffled crack and fiery pain leaped through his side as he curled up, trying to

156

protect himself.

From somewhere the she-demon had appeared. Donna kicking at Shelter, shrieking obscenities. She tried to kick him in the groin and succeeded in battering his thighs, his hands, his forearms. When that failed she flung herself on top of Morgan and ripped at his hair, his eyes, until Doran, fed up with the display, dragged her off of him.

"I'll kill him!" the woman screamed. "Give me a gun."

"No," Doran said coldly. "Panther will take care of that—and much more slowly and painfully than you would do it."

"It won't do you any good to kill me." Morgan got to hands and knees and then stood shakily, wiping back his dark hair. "You poor dumb bastard, you've lost the game, don't you understand that?"

"Shut up."

"I'm not the only one who knows what's going on here, not now." No, there was Boomer . . . and if they caught her it was all up. Let Doran worry, though, let him develop some doubts. Panther's mind was soaking this in.

Shelter went on. "The army knows you're a bogus officer. Shirke has been notified. Ball should be back there now with the information."

"Who are you?" Doran asked in a strangled whisper. "You're no scout, no wandering gunman who's stumbled onto this."

Morgan told him the truth. Even on his own lips it sounded strange. "Shelter Morgan. I'm a colonel in the U.S. army, working with a team of special investigators. My commanding officer is Major General Adolph Pomfret. Yes, he knows about this too. Just how long did you think you could keep this a secret? All of your hired

157

guns don't have closed mouths, you know. Star Dan knew. A man named Pablo Ruiz knows. My superior officer knows. By now Captain Shirke knows. By now he's headed this way with three companies of soldiers."

All of it was a lie, but it gave Doran plenty to think about. Panther actually looked worried. Shelter helped him to worry a little more.

"You'll be hung, Doran. Likely your sister will be too. Panther will be shot. His people will land right back on the reservation. If any of you have any sense you'll take off right now. There's nothing left for you to win, but plenty left to lose.

Panther looked questioningly at Doran. "If the army comes and my people do not have the new rifles . . ."

"He's lying, can't you see that!"

"And what if he is not?" Panther asked. "No matter, we will find out if he lies or not."

"Kill him," Donna kept saying as if it were some black prayer.

"No," Panther said, "not until he speaks the truth. And you will speak the truth," the renegade said, yanking Shelter's head around. "You *will.*"

Speaking rapidly to his men Panther went out. Morgan was dragged to his feet and carried out of the tipi into the fire-scented night. Campfires blazed away, smoke drifting on the wind through the night camp of the renegades.

Panther had promised to get the truth out of Morgan and Shelter had no idea that he wouldn't, given enough time, but time was the important element here. Time for Boomer to get away, time for her to reach Fort Randall. Time was the last gift Shelter had to give to the girl and to the settlers along Little Trace.

158

They already had it set up. Maybe it had been well-used.

Two upright poles with a cross-pole lashed to them stood before Morgan as his captors dragged him forward. Beneath the upright his shirt was ripped from his back and his hands lashed to the pole. His toes barely reached the ground, just enough so that he could touch the earth, but not enough so that he could take the strain off his shoulder joints.

The Cheyenne were gathering around, yelling, pointing, joking. Nothing like a free night's entertainment. Panther said something to his men and in a minute two of them were back with burning brands. Morgan felt hatred and despair mingle in his heart. They weren't going to waste any time and he had no doubt that in the end he would tell them the truth—or never speak again.

"Come on," Doran said sharply to Donna.

"I want to see it," she answered in a voice husky with emotion—sexual emotion.

"I said come on!" Doran yanked her around by the wrist. Morgan's eyes were directly on the renegade soldier's.

"I'll kill you. If I have to crawl back out of a grave to do it, Doran, I'll find you and kill you and it will make whatever the Indians do to me look like fun and games—"

The burning brand was laid across the flesh on Morgan's back and he screamed with pain. He could smell his own hide burning. The pain was indescribable, wave after wave of it sweeping across his body, surging volcanically into his skull.

Doran was smirking as he backed away, his lips moving

with unheard words. Donna was laughing out loud, hysterically laughing. Then they were gone and there was only the night, the fire, the Indians, and the pain.

Fire touched flesh again and Morgan felt the big darkness coming on. He drifted down into a tunnel filled with soft dark fire where there was no pain at all.

And no hope at all.

They brought him around sometime later by throwing water over his body. Morgan's teeth chattered violently. The night was cold and he was shirtless, soaked through. Then the fiery pain came back and he yelled out loud.

Panther stood before him. "You were lying, weren't you? No one else knows what has happened here. Only you."

"They know. The army'll be here soon. Run . . . get into the badlands and hide. Your war's over. There are no guns."

Panther spat into his face and nodded at the warriors around him. As their chief swept away they moved in again. A short warrior with an arrow in hand stepped to Morgan and slashed at his belly. Blood began to trickle down into his waistband. Morgan managed to get a boot up and smash it into the Indian's face and he fell back with a broken nose as the others laughed.

Then Shelter felt the heat nearing his back and the sudden searing pain as a brand was laid on his flesh over the old burns. He went out again, thankfully, tumbling through the familiar tunnel once more.

When he came around it was the middle of the night. A groan rose from his throat but he stifled it. He opened his swollen eyes a crack, seeing two warriors sitting near him, one by each upright. Apart from those two the camp seemed asleep.

A pony not far away shifted its feet and blew through its nostrils, and one of the guards lifted his head. He glanced back at Morgan and lowered his head once more.

No, Shelter hadn't gone anywhere. He was still hanging there like dead meat hung out to dry. His shoulders ached, his belly was a knot of pain. His back burned horribly as if they still held fire to it.

Peering up cautiously Shelter looked at the criss-crossed ties which held his hands to the cross-pole. The knots were secure and tight. He wasn't going to slip them.

He next turned his attention to the lashes holding the cross-pole to the uprights. They seemed secure enough too, at least secure enough to hold his weight, but he wondered . . .

Shelter lifted his feet from the ground and the pole sagged an inch or so. When he pushed off again with his toes the pole lifted three or four inches, and he thought he felt some movement up above. He looked at his guard and saw no reaction to this slight movement, and so he tested it again. Pushing off with his toes, sagging down, pushing upward again. The pole lifted slightly, definitely, and Morgan smiled through bruised and bloodied lips.

Hell, it wasn't much of a chance, but he had absolutely none where he was. He wasn't going to willingly let them brand him again. Maybe the last prisoner hadn't been quite so tall as the lean Tennessean. Maybe no one had ever thought of it before, or lasted long enough to give it a try—but Morgan thought he had one slender chance.

He glanced again at his guards and then carefully began his movement again, sagging down and then pushing off with his feet. This time, however, it was no tentative movement, but a last desperate gamble for life, and when he pushed upward he did it with all the strength

161

of his long thighs and hard-muscle calves. The first time was a miss. The second thrust of his long legs lifted the cross-pole off the uprights and sent Morgan crashing to the ground.

The guard to his right was the first one to come alert, and with all of the fury pent up inside him Shell swung the end of the long pole around, smashing the teeth from the renegade's face, sending him sprawling to the ground.

Immediately Shelter swung back the other way, and the guard to his left took a blow to the throat from the ten-foot-long pole. It smashed his windpipe and left him gagging for breath on the dark earth.

Shelter never saw him hit the ground. He was sprinting toward the Indian pony he had spotted nearby. He went up over the haunches, still strapped tightly to the pole, and heeled the startled animal into sudden motion.

Then he was racing from the camp, a single wild shot following him through the darkness.

He reached the timber and was torn from the horse's back as the pole caught the trunk of a pine. Bleeding from the face and arms Morgan got furiously, hastily, to his feet, and with the pole held out before him, he smashed it repeatedly against the tree until it snapped into two equal sections. Tearing the broken pole free from its rawhide ties Shelter found the Indian pony and again mounted it, urging it on wildly through the night while behind him war whoops sounded.

14.

The rain began to fall again, and the big man with the scars on his back, with the open festering wound on his belly, rode on through the darkness toward the Tangles, knowing that a hundred renegade raiders were looking for him, that ahead somewhere a mercenary army would welcome him gladly into their bloody arms.

And that somewhere out there a little red-headed girl with a heart full of love and a body alive with sexual want was trying to fight her way toward freedom.

Shelter held the Indian pony up at the little creek and swung down to stand on wobbly legs as the horse drank. Scooping mud from the riverbank he daubed it on the burn wounds on his back as best he could, cooling the heat that tormented his body only a little.

He soaked his rawhide-burned hands in the icy water and tried to clean the tear across his abdomen a little. Then he stood, and sucking in the cold air deeply, he looked up the backtrail wondering if he had lost them.

Somehow he doubted it. There was a sliver of a pale moon rising; not enough for most men to see their feet by, but plenty for a good Cheyenne tracker to follow sign across the roughest ground in God's roughest country.

163

"It's not good," he muttered to the horse, which pricked its ears curiously.

No, it wasn't good. Unarmed, surrounded by enemies, lost in hostile territory, it was very bad indeed. What a man does then—a real man—is go on. Fight it through. You don't sit down and cry and give up and curse the fates that have brought you there. Morgan swung wearily aboard the stolen Indian pony and went on, walking the pony up the creek to hide his tracks as well as possible.

He was near the Tangles, he knew, but that knowledge did him little good. He thought it was possible to hide out there, but hiding out wasn't what he needed now. He had to get to Fort Randall, had to find Boomer, and that meant riding across miles of open country without so much as a knife to keep his pursuers off his back.

They were back there now.

Someone was back there. Pulling his horse to the side, out of the creek, he sat and listened to the night sounds. The wind in the pines, the distant call of an owl. And the sounds of a horse carefully placing its feet. If he could hear them, they could hear him, but he couldn't sit where he was. Angling up higher into the timber Morgan half-turned in the saddle as he rode, but he saw nothing. Not just then.

He crested a small dark knoll. Beyond, the Tangles lay in the thin light of the moon. An eerie wilderness, ravaged by some giant in time beyond memory. A place God had forgotten to touch.

The Cheyenne came up out of the ground and his hatchet chopped at Shelter Morgan's head. Shell could see his eyes, hard and bright, could see moonlight on the hatchet head.

He kicked out of the stirrups, blocking the violent

164

downward blow with his crossed wrists catching the Indian's forearm. Still the hatchet nicked him and Morgan, falling, felt hot blood trickling down his arm.

The horse reared up and Morgan rolled under it, going toward the renegade's knees. He landed solidly against the Indian's legs and the Cheyenne went reeling back, his head striking hard against the ground as the horse cantered off, tossing its head.

The hatchet had flown free, and as the Cheyenne reached for it Morgan threw an elbow into the warrior's throat. Still the Indian, wheezing as he tried to breathe, fought back and Shelter, pinning his shoulders with his knees, hammered blow after blow into the renegade's face until he lay still and bloody against the earth.

Shelter stepped back panting. The renegade didn't have much Morgan could use. Apparently he was one of those waiting for Doran's rifles. Morgan took the hatchet, placing it behind his belt, and swung aboard his horse again, heading for the Tangles, wondering where that little red-headed woman had gotten to—and if she was even alive on this cold dark night.

They weren't going to give it up. An hour on, Morgan was sure that he again had renegade Cheyenne on his trail. More than one this time. Now and then he heard an owl hoot from the Tangles, but it wasn't an owl.

They were ahead of him and behind him. Maybe they had found his tracks. It was possible; the night had grown clear, the slender rising moon brighter against the stars.

Shelter rode through the badlands carefully as he had to. Picking his way over the acres of fallen trees that lay scattered like bones, winding up the dark canyons deep in moonshadow. The horse was tiring now, shuffling over the sandy earth.

When the shot came from out of the darkness, the muzzle flash was so close that it blinded Shell temporarily even as he hurled himself from the saddle, to roll and run, rifle fire following him as he wound through the rocks and trees, running like a madman, weaving to keep the marksmen off their target.

Three staccato shots struck near him, too near, ripping at the dead trees, whining off the granite of the bluff before him. Morgan went to the ground again.

The first renegade was too confident, too intent on taking Morgan's scalp.

The Indian leaped a tree, firing as he came, and by the muzzle flash Shelter saw clearly the look of triumph on the warrior's face.

That look didn't last long.

Morgan had one weapon, one chance. He took the hatchet from his belt and balanced it in his hand. The Indian was no more than twenty feet away when Shelter sent it spinning through the air. Honed steel bit into the Indian's face, cleaving the skull as his rifle spat aimless flame.

Still the renegade ran toward Shell, his legs wobbly now, his face smeared with hot blood. He dropped nearly at Morgan's feet, and his outstretched hand seemed to offer his weapon to Morgan as a gift of victory.

Morgan snatched up the rifle and levered through three rounds at the oncoming renegades, feeling the dead Indian's blood against his cheek as he sighted.

The answering fire backed the renegades away quickly. One bullet tagged flesh with a solid thump and a man grunted with pain. Then the night was still again and Shelter patted the Indian down, finding a buckskin sack filled with spare cartridges. He wasn't going to sit there

166

and trade fire with the renegades, and so, looking up, he began trying to make his way up the bluff.

Rifle fire searched for him, whining off the rock face of the low bluff as Morgan climbed one-handed. No way the rifle was going to be left behind. That was wrapped firmly in his left hand. The last shot as he rolled up and over to the flat of the rim tugged at Morgan's sleeve, missing only by that much.

Shelter crept back from the rim and started jogging across the mesa. The Indians wouldn't be far behind. They knew how much taking Shelter down meant.

He was the man who knew too much. If Panther didn't totally trust Doran, at least Doran was a hope for a future, land for his people, arms to build up a powerful army that could hold off the American incursions. Doran was strength and wealth and power. Morgan was the lone man who could tear down the dream castles Panther was building in his mind and in the minds of his people.

They would come.

Morgan kept going—deeper into the Tangles. He didn't want to lead the renegades toward Boomer. Yet at some point he was going to have to turn west and make his way toward Fort Randall. Afoot again it was going to be slow traveling.

Shelter glanced skyward. The moon was well along in its descent. Sunrise couldn't be far off. That was all he needed. Shelter paused, caught his breath, and stood looking down into another twisting valley.

Then he saw them and he hit the ground fast. Four Cheyenne raiders were walking their horses along the valley floor, searching for sign. Terrific. Now they had him cut off. The renegades he had encountered back there would be climbing the bluff, following him. They would come a little more cautiously now, but they would be coming all the same.

Morgan backed away from the bluff's edge and began to circle the mesa, looking for a safe way down if such a thing existed.

The moon faded and it grew darker. If he hadn't found a way off by sunrise, there was every chance he would never do it. He started thinking about trying to hole up, moving out again the next night. Two problems. First, he would be wasting time he couldn't afford to lose, and second, there didn't seem to be any place a man could hide.

Scattered cedars, wind-bent, occasional stacks of weathered boulders across mostly barren, broken ground. He was just going to have to go on with this deadly game of hide-and-seek.

Shelter ripped off a section of his shirttail and fashioned a crude sling for the rifle. He looked over the edge of the bluff and sucked in his breath. It was going to be a hell of a job getting down even with both hands free.

And if his luck had turned sour he might just find himself reaching the bottom to find the renegades already there. There wasn't much choice. He started down.

Easing over the rim of the bluff he searched for a foothold, finding only a narrow, foot-long ridge. He tested it, found it would hold his weight, and eased on over. Using the ridge as a handhold he lowered himself again, inching his way down the bluff, knowing that if they spotted him hung up there he was a goner.

Shelter was bathed in sweat before he reached the floor of the canyon. He froze suddenly, turning. The sound of horses' hoofs against the sand was clear if faint in the night. There was a clump of greasewood just behind him and Morgan took to its meager cover. He sat and waited, rifle in his hands, his back pressed to the bluff, eyes straining through the screen of brush.

They came on slowly, four of them. Whether they were the same four he had seen earlier, he couldn't tell. Morgan pressed back into the shadows. Sweat trickled into his eyes. They were near enough that he could see the markings of their horses now. If the moon had been just a little higher, they would have had him . . . and they might yet.

Shelter's hand was cramped around the rifle, his thumb glued to the hammer. How many could he take if it came down to it? Two, three? Only with great luck, and those who were left would gun him down, savaging his body later, leaving his flesh to the critters, his bones to bleach like the dead trees in the Tangles.

They were going to go past. Morgan's heart was hammering away. He held his breath. *Go on*, he urged them silently. There was a small chance he might get away with it after all. He had left no tracks for them to find. They couldn't know where he was.

Just as he thought that, one of the renegades shouted out and Morgan started to come up with the rifle. A voice answered the renegade's cry. From atop the mesa someone called down.

Sweat ran down Shelter's arms despite the cold. The two forces had found each other again. They had Morgan between them but didn't know it! The two parties talked for a while and Shelter started to get itchy. The longer the renegades sat there, the better their chance of spotting Shelter in the brush.

It went on for long minutes that seemed like hours.

Finally one of the mounted men laughed, raised a hand, and the four of them started on. Shelter watched them go. From above, pebbles and sand trickled down into his face as he looked up, trying to get some clue as to what they were up to.

More time passed. The sliver of a moon went down behind the hills and there was a dull gray light in the eastern sky. Shelter couldn't wait any longer.

He rose slowly, keeping his eyes on the rim above which now stood out starkly against the paling sky. Then he started on, back down the canyon, moving in the opposite direction of the renegade patrol—and deeper into the Tangles.

The sand was flushed with early color now. The bizarre forms of the Tangles began to take on definition. No good. This was no good. He was going to have to hole up, like it or not. He paused, looking around. The land looked vaguely familiar but only vaguely.

What he saw next stopped his heart.

A torn piece of cloth clung to the sage beside the trail. Morgan went to it, taking it from the brush. It was Boomer's. It matched her shirt too well.

Looking around more carefully Shelter found the indistinct, very small set of footprints in the sand. It looked as if she had fallen and gotten to her feet again. Shelter found the man's tracks next and he cursed slowly.

They had her.

He started following. There was nothing else to do. He lost the tracks in a rock-strewn reddish arroyo and picked them up again a few hundred yards on. Boomer seemed to be dazed or very reluctant—the tracks indicated she was being half-dragged along.

But where was she being taken? Looking upcountry Morgan couldn't figure it. There was no way out of there and back to the outlaw camp. Or none that he knew of. He wiped his cuff across his forehead and started on once more.

The country got a hell of a lot rougher and the sun got hotter. Morgan didn't think he had the renegades on his backtrail anymore, but he couldn't be sure, and he spent a lot of time stopping, looking back, watching the shifting shadows across the silent land, listening for a telltale sound like a hoof on stone.

There was cholla cactus everywhere now and some nopal. Outside of these nothing seemed to live here in the red earth country of the badlands. The land itself was cut by abruptly appearing gorges and sawtooth ridges.

Morgan was penetrating deeper and deeper into rough country, alone, hunted, without water or food, and he didn't like it at all. He liked the idea of Boomer being someone's prisoner a lot less. Her tracks were still occasionally visible on the hard ground, and once Morgan found a few knotted strands of red hair where she had ducked to go under a long-dead low-hanging cedar tree.

He reached the summit finally and stopped, breathing deeply. His feet burned, his knees were raw from a fall he had taken. His mouth was dry for want of water. The badlands stretched out in all directions and the wind gusted across the crest.

He heard the rifle behind him cocking before he heard so much as a footstep. He turned slowly, very slowly.

"You track pretty good for a white man," Pablo Ruiz said.

"Where's Boomer?"

"I got her. She's a little hurt."

"How little?"

Ruiz lowered his rifle. "Arrow grazed her thigh. Not bad, but she's got a fever, lost some blood."

"What are you doing way the hell out here?" Morgan asked.

"Things are pretty hot back there," the Mexican-Indian said, nodding eastward, "or didn't you notice?"

"I noticed."

"I come up deeper in the Tangles. Figured no one would bother me out here. What the hell they want to come up here for? Just to kill me? I ain't worth it."

"Where's Boomer."

"I'll show you." He glanced down at the rifle. "Sorry about that. I didn't recognize you from behind and I'm not taking many chances out here."

"Don't blame you. Show me the girl."

Ruiz hesitated a minute and then nodded, leading the way. He had taken some dead cedar poles and placed them across a cut in the rocks. Into these he had woven sagebrush and greasewood, making a little lean-to for himself. Very primitive, but it would keep Ruiz out of the weather and that was all he seemed to want.

Boomer was inside.

"How you doing, kid?" Morgan asked, crouching down beside her to touch her forehead. Fevered eyes came open and she clutched Shelter's hand.

"I let you down, tall man."

"Hell—how were you supposed to keep from getting hurt? I'm just glad you're alive."

"And you . . . how did you get out alive, Shelter? God, I worried about you."

"A long story. I got lucky. How's your leg? Hurt?"

172

"Plenty. Pablo patched me up a little, but it hurts."

"Take a look? Shell asked. At her nod he pulled the blanket up and studied the wound in her thigh. It wasn't bad, but anytime someone punches a hunk of flesh out of you it hurts, and if you don't have a doctor, soap, hot water, or bandages you've got a problem. "Just too bad they had to get such a pretty part," Morgan said and Boomer smiled weakly.

"Shell, what are we going to do?"

"About what?"

"The army. The ranchers in the valley. *Dad*."

"I'll try to get through, I guess. If Pablo can take of you for a little longer.

"No, Shell," the lady said, "I'm going too."

"Like hell. How're you going to travel?"

"I can make it, honest, Shelter."

"Sure."

"Pablo's got a mule. He'll let me take it, won't you, Pablo?"

The Indian nodded but Shelter still shook his head. "It won't be much easier on you riding than walking. Besides, if you think that mule is going to outrun any Indian ponies, you're crazy."

"That mule," Pablo said, "outrun anything. Run all day, all night."

"Anything but a bullet, right, Pablo?"

The Indian made an indefinite gesture. Shelter turned back to Boomer, "It won't work, kid."

"But you can just walk out of here, run back to Randall, and take care of it all alone, right?" She had her temper back. She wasn't *that* sick. "Look, it's no good for me to lay out here on the ground and you know it. Think I'm better off here, Shelter, really?"

She did have a point. Morgan looked around the lean-to and then at Ruiz. "Lady, out there they want to kill us."

"Yeah."

"We can only be lucky so many times."

"Yeah."

"I can't say anything to talk you out of this, can I, Boomer?"

"No."

"And there's nothing I can do."

"Sure," she said brightly. "Hand me my pants and turn your back."

174

15.

The long-eared long-jointed buckskin mule stepped out briskly across the badlands. It minded the reins—barely—but seemed to have an active disdain for the judgment of human passengers and preferred to pick its own way.

Boomer rode, and from time to time Shelter climbed up behind her when his legs began to knot. They saw no signs of human beings, no smoke, no color, no reflected light, but neither of them was lulled into a false sense of security. Panther hadn't found them yet, but it was unlikely he would quit until he had or until they rode that cantankerous mule through the gates of Fort Randall.

Riding behind Boomer had its advantages. There wasn't much to hold onto, but what there was, was interesting. Shelter let his hand ride up under her shirt and cup her firm, full breast, or he dipped it around to hold her crotch. Pleasant as that was, this was no Sunday picnic ride, and he jerked himself back to alertness constantly. He wasn't going to do himself or Boomer any good if he didn't keep his eyes moving, stay awake to the real possibility that Panther's raiders might rise up out of the ground at any moment.

They got a break late that afternoon—it began to rain again, very hard. It made for miserable going, but the visibility dropped to almost nothing, screening them from searching eyes.

The mule simply plodded on.

"He know where he's going?" Shelter asked.

"I guess he's heading back toward the old cave where Pablo used to hole up. That'll suit us fine. We can get up across the mesa and drop down into Little Trace again."

"*If* he knows where he's going," Morgan said, shouting above the sound of the hard rain.

Boomer turned her head. "Want to go on ahead and scout the way for us, tall man?"

Morgan just laughed, gave her a squeeze, and hung on. She was probably right about the mule heading back to its former home. At any rate they were heading east still. The wind out of the north was constant on Shelter's left cheek.

If Boomer was in a lot of pain she didn't let on, and knowing her she wouldn't. Twice Morgan made her get down and rest the leg, but she finally convinced him that it was just as uncomfortable as riding.

The day cleared and grew warmer. It seemed they had somehow done the impossible and lost the renegades. Shelter could spot no one on their tail. They achieved the mesa and rode across it through the pines toward Little Trace, and Boomer finally let out the sigh of relief she'd been holding in for so long.

"It's all right," she said. "They didn't come."

The little ranch house was still standing and Kennedy was in his field working. He looked up as the mule approached, paused as if thunderstruck, and then, grinning, walked to help his daughter from the mule.

"One day I'll whip your butt so you'll never sit again," Kennedy said, but he didn't mean a word of it. He hugged Boomer and saw her wince. "What's the matter, honey?"

"Nothing. I got nicked," she answered.

"Nicked?" Kennedy looked at Shelter.

"She belongs in bed," Morgan said. "The both of you belong in Rosalia if you ask me."

"I told you I'm not pulling out," Kennedy said stiffly. "I'll not give up my land and house."

"Then you'll just have to stay here, Boomer. You can't ride anymore," Morgan said.

"Bull." Shelter had run into a stubborn clan. "I'm going with you. I'll take Dad's sorrel. All right, Dad?"

"It's all right . . . but where are you going, Boomer?" The old man scratched his head.

"Morgan wants me to go somewhere safe. I'm going to Fort Randall with him."

"Boomer . . ." Shell objected. It was still a long and dangerous ride ahead of them.

"Besides, I need a doctor. You said so yourself." Boomer was triumphant. "They've got one at the fort."

"What is this 'nick' of yours?" Kennedy asked. His worry was showing a little.

"Ah, just this." Boomer hiked her skirt and showed her father her thigh. "Renegade arrow, I guess."

"Woman . . . how did I spawn a wild thing like you, Boomer Kennedy? Out there fighting Indians and such." Kennedy's worry deepened, but there was simultaneous pride in his eyes.

"Maybe it is best if she goes on to the fort," Morgan commented. "There's no way of telling where the renegades are, no way of telling where a person is safe."

"I'd tell her what to do," Kennedy said sourly, "but I reckon she'll do as she pleases anyway. Go on, Boomer, take the sorrel." She started away, limping, but he called her back. "Boomer!" Kennedy just tapped his cheek and, smiling, she went to tiptoes and kissed him there before hurrying away again.

"I got work to do," Kennedy muttered. Shaking his head he got back to his team and plow.

Shelter just had time to dip some water from the bucket at the well before Boomer returned with the saddled sorrel. She ducked inside the house, returning with some stale cornbread and a plate of cold beans.

"That's all there was. Dad's no cook. He eats what I've made until it's gone and then quits eating."

There was a tinge of regret in her eyes as she looked at her father. The two of them really loved each other in their rough, undemonstrative way. Morgan shoveled the food into his face. Anything would have been good to eat at that point.

Boomer ate something hastily herself and took Shell's plate into the house. Returning she had a rifle under her arm. "Missed having a little security," she muttered. She checked the action and loaded the Winchester.

Then, lifting her hand to her father, she got gingerly aboard the sorrel and led the way out of the yard, Morgan following on the stolid buckskin mule.

Luck was with them. For hour after hour they saw no other riders on the long plains, and by the time they reached Randall in late afternoon Shelter finally let out his own long sigh of relief.

"Made it, kid," Shelter said.

"Yeah, made it. Shelter—there's still an army of raiders out there. What have we gained?"

178

"We know what we're fighting, Boomer. We know *who*. And we know where the bastards are."

"And now someone's got to do some warring." She held up the sorrel and stretched out a hand to Morgan's. "Who? You, Shelter?"

"Maybe I'll give a hand. That's what they're paying me for."

"You got the wrong job, big man."

"Yeah," Shelter agreed, "maybe so."

Boomer protested, but Shelter took her into Rosalia and got her a room in the hotel. Then he sent the local doctor up. Captain Finney at the fort may have been just as good or better, but he hadn't had much practice with the female version of mankind.

Besides, the army might have use for its surgeon.

"You come back alive and well, you bastard," Boomer said before Shell left. The doctor blinked and glanced at her with surprise as he opened his bag.

"I'll be back. You know me, I'm indestructible."

"Prove it this time," Boomer said, and her eyes misted over a little. Shelter turned sharply away and went out, leaving the girl to the doctor's care.

It was nearly sundown when Shelter rode the lanky mule in through the gates of Fort Randall, but the captain was still in his office, staring at the wall, drinking, obviously worried. When Shelter entered his office he practically leaped to his feet.

"Colonel Morgan! I assumed by now . . ."

"They came close, but I'm still around," Shelter said with a grin and the captain smiled with relief. *"Now,"* Morgan told the officer, "I could use a drink."

There was a lot to talk about. As the captain poured Morgan a drink Shell laid it out as briefly as possible.

179

Shirke nearly spilt the whiskey when Shell named Doran as the traitor.

"He's just a boy!"

"A cunning boy, believe me."

Shirke downed his drink. "It seems incredible."

"Sorry, but it's so. His only reason for accepting an army commission was to further his plot. If you've got his personnel file it might be worth going through. It should show that he was the surveyor in charge of the mapping of the badlands."

"I seem to recall something about his having been a surveyor . . ." Shirke rubbed his temples. "But, damn it all! He's just a boy."

"Yeah. You know Harry Hodges is dead, I take it."

"Yes. I'm left with Ball and Michaelson. No one else. And Michaelson is still an office soldier, a storekeeper at the bottom." Shirke was juggling his manpower, trying to find a way to do what had to be done—what they both knew had to be done. Strike and strike hard. Now.

"If you've got a good field NCO you might consider a field promotion," Morgan suggested.

"Yes, yes. There's Cavendish." Shirke wrote himself a memo and then looked up as if startled. "The supposed army raiders?"

"Doran was the only man out there who was actually army. The rest were wearing uniforms, that's all."

"But how could they have gotten them?"

"Who's your supply sergeant?" Morgan asked.

"Just now we haven't one. We're short everywhere. Sergeant Stoner has been doubling in that department."

"I know. Doran told me."

"He what?" The captain's face fell.

"He told me that he'd paid Stoner to furnish uniforms.

Presumably with the idea of confusing things, getting any local settler who happened to witness a raid to distrust the army."

"Bill Stoner has twenty-eight years in the service!"

"Looking to retirement."

"Certainly."

"Apparently," Shell said, "Stoner didn't think the army was going to be paying him enough for his time."

"I can't accept that." Shirke shook his head heavily.

"You'd better. It's true. Stoner tried to set me up the first night I was here. He had someone try to kill me. After he tried to chase me off with a beating. He knew something, or smelled it, or was tipped off."

Shirke's voice was hoarse. "My God, it was my fault, wasn't it? The times I screwed up and called you 'sir' or 'Colonel.'"

"Not really. Tell me this," Shell said, putting his glass on the captain's desk, "who opens your mail? Dispatches, communiques from HQ?" He didn't really have to ask.

"Someone has to sort things out, of course," Shirke said in that same hoarse voice. "The first sergeant is normally responsible for that."

"Don't blame yourself then, Captain. He knew. That's the only way to explain his immediate animosity. He read the dispatches, told Doran, tried to have me killed knowing I could blow things up in his face."

"It's still hard to accept—Stoner." Shirke rubbed his forehead more vigorously now.

"Accept it. Check out those uniform requisitions for a start and then throw the bastard in the stockade."

"I'll have that done now, Colonel, if you're—"

"I'd like to talk to him first. If you'll tell me where

181

he is."

"I'll take you over there, sir."

"Alone," Morgan said. "I'd like to talk to Bill Stoner alone."

"If . . ." Whatever Shirke was going to say ended abruptly as he studied the hard, cold look in Morgan's eyes. "He's in his quarters. What do you want me to do, sir?"

"Call in Ball, Michaelson, and this Sergeant Cavendish. Brief them. Tell them we're moving out at first light. I'll be back to pinpoint the targets."

"Are you taking command?" Shirke asked. Morgan shook his head.

"This is yours, Captain. I'm going with you, but I'm leaving the troops to you."

"Why go, then?" Shirke rose, a half-smile on his thin lips. "You could certainly use some sleep, some food."

"That's right, I could. But there are a few personal scores wrapped up in this as well, sir."

"Doran?"

Morgan nodded without speaking. Then he turned and went out past the duty corporal, asking the way to Stoner's quarters. Shirke stood in the doorway, watching him go. Then he turned to his corporal. "I want Ball, Michaelson, and Sergeant Cavendish in my office in ten minutes. *Ten.*"

The door banged open and slammed against the wall, and Sergeant Bill Stoner, top dog on this post, leaped out of his bunk with a roar of anger.

"Who in hell . . . !"

Then he knew who in hell, and he shut his mouth,

backing away a step as the unshaven, blue-eyed man crossed the room toward him. "Hello, Stoner."

"Morgan, you're . . ."

"No, I'm not dead. No thanks to you and Doran. But you've had all the chances you're going to get, Stoner. You're going to miss out on the big money Doran promised you. You're going to miss out on your pension. Hell, you're going to miss out on living if I have anything to say about it. I don't like greedy men, I don't like men who'll sell their own up the creek, who'll turn traitor for a few bucks."

"So what're you going to do?" Stoner asked, and Shelter saw his eyes shift slightly toward the bunk.

"The first thing I'm going to do is kick your ass, Stoner. I at least want that pleasure. Then I'm going to see if we can find six men for a firing squad."

"Like hell, you bastard!" Stoner dove for his bunk, but Morgan had anticipated something like that and he was quicker than the fat first sergeant. When Stoner came out from under the pillow with his service revolver in his hand, Shell was in his face and as he slapped Stoner's wrist away he leveled a punch at the big man's jaw which sent him staggering back into the wall.

Stoner's pistol lay on the floor as his head cracked against the wall and he started to slide down. Shell kicked it aside and moved in again.

Stoner didn't have character but he had some balls. He bunched his fists, bowed his neck, and charged at Morgan. Shell kicked him hard on the kneecap and then planted a stiff left in the sergeant's face.

"You tried this before, Stoner. Didn't work, did it? It's not going to work now. I'm going to leave you in a puddle on the floor."

183

"You son of a bitch," Stoner managed to pant. "Kill you."

Stoner came in again, his mouth twisted open with rage. Shelter stabbed that left into the NCO's face again and then hooked with a right that caught Stoner on the throat.

But Stoner came on, wrapping his massive arms around Shell, pinning his arms, squeezing with all he had, forcing the breath from Morgan until Shell banged down hard with his forehead and Stoner fell back with a howl, his nose hanging from shattered bone.

Morgan had no mercy in him. He moved in. A left to the ribs took the wind from Stoner and if Shell's next left missed the ducking sergeant, the right that followed didn't.

It was flush to the jaw and the big man tottered on his feet for a long moment, his eyes glazing over before he hit the deck. Morgan stepped back to let the man fall flat on his battered face. Then, yanking Stoner's body up by the collar, he dragged him out into the night.

Lieutenant Ball was there, hurrying toward the commander's office, and he pulled up short, muttering a curse. "You! Who's that, Stoner? What in hell are you doing?"

Ball drew his pistol from his holster and cocked it. "Straight ahead, Morgan. That's right. The captain's office."

Shelter didn't bother to answer. That was where Stoner was going all right. In through the orderly room, past the startled eyes of the duty corporal and into Shirke's office, where he dropped Stoner to the floor again.

Shirke shot up behind his desk, his gray face flushing.

The balding Lieutenant Michaelson, very sleepy, shook his head in disbelief. A blond NCO Morgan hadn't seen before started toward him, fire in his eyes.

Shirke bellowed, "Lieutenant Ball! Lower that weapon you have trained on Colonel Morgan."

"*Colonel . . . ?*" Ball's voice was a mousy little squeak. He looked at the gun in his hand as if it had betrayed him.

"I am sorry, sir," Shirke said to Shelter, "but it seems the time for secrecy is past. Besides . . ."

"He wouldn't have shot," Morgan said. "Beat me, maybe. Handcuffed me, but he wouldn't have shot me, would you, Ball?"

"No, sir," Ball whispered, his mind still groping, trying to assimilate this new and improbable information. On the floor Stoner groaned, and Shelter Morgan kicked him hard in the head. Ball flinched and the captain muttered, "Jesus."

"Put irons on this man, Captain," Shell said. "And keep them on. Take possession of the key yourself. Then lock him up in the darkest corner of that stockade."

"Yes," Shirke said quietly. "Corporal!" He called his duty corporal in and give him instructions. The corporal's face was as uncomprehending as Ball's.

"I can't understand this," Ball finally said. "What is happening?"

"Simple." Morgan turned on him. "Stoner's a renegade, selling out soldiers for money. He wasn't alone. There's a man in the officer ranks."

"Not me!" Ball practically screamed. "Sir, I swear it."

"I didn't think it was you," Morgan said. "You're a bastard, officious and self-centered, a little Napoleon who needs to straighten himself up or get his butt out of

185

the army, but you aren't the one."

Morgan told them who it was and then went on to explain again what was happening upcountry. Shirke slumped in his chair, the others shook their heads or stood staring in disbelief.

"Well?" It was Michaelson who spoke. "What do we do now, sir?"

"Now," Morgan said, "we kick ass."

"But if they have Panther . . . all those hired guns . . ."

"I didn't say we went to Sunday tea, Lieutenant, I said we kick ass. They're not going to give us anything. But we're going to take it all the same. There'll be blood on the plains and there'll be a few widows sitting staring out the door for a man who's never coming back, but we *will* kick ass. Captain," Morgan said, turning his head to watch as Stoner was dragged from the room by three armed soldiers, "I'll leave the details to you."

"And you, sir?"

Morgan astonished him by winking. "I'm going to get some sleep. If there's some ass-kicking to do, I'm going to be there and I'm going to be ready."

186

16.

They rode out with the dawn, a long line of blue-clad men, anxious and tense. At the point rode the cavalry captain and the tall man in buckskin trousers and dark blue shell shirt. Shirke had asked him about a uniform, but Morgan had just smiled.

"The last uniform I had was gray, Captain, and there wasn't a hell of a lot left of that when I was through with it."

Shirke just fell silent, figuring, Morgan supposed, that if Major General Pomfret had wanted him to know why his men didn't wear uniforms he would have been told.

Right.

Lieutenant Ball rode up beside Shelter and he glanced at him. On that pinched face there was some anxiety, some hostility.

"I didn't really have the chance to apologize to you, sir," Ball said.

"No need."

"But there is. I just didn't know who you are, you see," Ball went on. "If I had . . ."

"You're apologizing for the wrong reason, Ball," Shelter told the officer.

"Sir?"

"You're apologizing for the sake of your career. I don't give a damn about your career one way or the other. I'm the most irregular colonel you're going to run into. Believe it or not, I was drafted into this army—that's right, a full colonel drafted. It's a long story and I don't want to go into it now."

Ball didn't have a clue as to what Shelter was talking about. "I only tried to do my duty, sir. Now I am apologizing for what was obviously a mistake in judgment."

"You don't get me, do you, Ball?" Shelter asked. "Your apology is accepted. I really don't care. I've got other things on my mind right now."

"I realize that, sir, but—"

"But you shouldn't suddenly be sorry just because you found out that I was a superior officer. You should be sorry because you treated a *man* badly."

Ball stiffened and began another apology. Shelter cut the officer off. "From what I've seen you're not much better with your own subordinates. Again, I really don't care. I'm not writing up any reports, I'm not rating your efficiency. I'm just telling you for your own sake as well as that of others. Look, Ball, there's too many men who carry a saber or a badge or a piece of paper who think it gives them the right to ride roughshod over others. It doesn't work that way. A man has dignity and you have to respect it. It doesn't matter if it's the greenest boot in your company. Give him some respect and you'll get some back. You'll get more—loyalty, a willingness to fight for the man in command. Believe me.

"Have you wondered why a man like Henry Hodges got respect from his troops?"

Ball waved a hand. "Well, naturally, he was an enlisted man. He came from the same place as the others."

"Yeah, from his momma's womb, my friend. Same place we all came from. Now he's gone to the same place we all go. But his men remember him. They don't say, 'Good, the bastard's gone.' How do you think your people will feel if you catch a slug today, Ball? No, you owe someone an apology, but it's not me. It's not me."

Ball swung his horse away. He still couldn't figure it, and Shell doubted he ever would.

The Indian scout, Walika, was riding in hard and Captain Shirke held up the column as Morgan rode to the point to wait for the Delaware.

"Panther," Walika said before his horse had come to a stop. He pointed toward the Tangles, his chest rising and falling beneath his buckskin shirt. "He comes out to meet us."

"You're sure?" Shirke asked needlessly. "How far ahead, Walika?"

"Two miles, maybe."

"Colonel?"

"I told you it was your battle to win, Captain."

"If we could be sure . . ." Shirke looked around uncertainly. "On the flats we have the numbers to take him. If he stays in the Tangles, I don't know. I don't want to ride into an ambush."

Again Shirke looked at Morgan for help, but Shelter's job wasn't to substitute for a combat officer when things got hairy. Maybe, looking at Shirke again, at the pallor and tightness of his face, he was going to have to do it though.

"How about sending out a patrol?" Shelter suggested. "See what kind of fire they draw."

"Yes," Shirke said. "All right." What was it with Shirke? Age, the bottle, too much time behind a desk? It didn't matter. Shelter wasn't going to let the raiders off the hook, and if he had to play soldier he'd do it.

"I'll take your acting lieutenant, Sergeant Cavendish," Morgan said, weighing the alternatives—Michaelson, who was willing but inexperienced, Ball who was experienced but abrasive. "Give us ten men and let us test the waters."

"*You*, Colonel?"

"Yeah. Me, colonel," Shelter answered, unlimbering his Winchester repeater.

Shirke motioned Cavendish forward and the NCO, his hair graying, red face set, came forward. "Sergeant, you're mounting a patrol with Colonel Morgan. Pick ten men."

"Yes, sir."

"Good luck, Morgan," Shirke said. "Do you have a suggestion for my deployment?"

Shelter looked to the high ground of the mesa above them. "A picket line up there. If we come riding out of the Tangles with a hundred Cheyenne on our butts you'll be able to flank them. If that happens, Shirke, don't save any ammunition for tomorrow. Otherwise—send a courier in to find us . . . I'd guess Walika would be the best for that job."

"Yes, sir," Shirke said, obviously relieved that Morgan was taking command. "Morgan—you were in the war." "The war" meant only one—the War Between the States.

"I was in it."

"Cavalry?" Shirke asked.

"That's right. Infantry first, then cavalry when they

190

gave me a commission and could spare a horse."

"You were on the Rebel side."

Shelter's eyes narrowed a little. He didn't like the term "Rebel" much. "Yeah, that's right."

"I was in it," Shirke said as if distantly recalling events. "Artillery, sir. I'm afraid those skills haven't done much for me out here. Artillery is generally useless against the Indians. I'm a career soldier. I do my best."

"Yes?" Cavendish was back with his chosen men.

"I suppose I'm apologizing," Shirke said with his eyes still distant, his head hanging a little. Everyone was apologizing to Shelter today, it seemed. None of it meant a thing.

"Forget it," he replied. "No one is everything. I won't apologize for not being able to sing a note or juggle. So long as you'll *fight*, Shirke."

"Sir!" The captain stiffened with indignation. "I will fight to the best of my ability so long as I am physically able."

Shelter grinned. "Then you're a soldier. Forget the rest of the crap. Ready, Cavendish?"

"Ready, sir."

They rode slowly toward the Tangles while Shirke turned his column toward the highlands. Cavendish grinned at Morgan.

"Moved up kind of fast, didn't you, scout?"

"I apply myself."

"Glad to hear it. You do know what we're doing, don't you? Riding into the face of a hundred renegades."

"Don't forget the white raiders" Morgan said.

"No," Cavendish answered. "I haven't forgotten. It's them I'd like to get my hands on. Panther, I can kind of understand. The whites—I don't get it."

191

"Understand greed and you've got it," Morgan answered.

"Is it true—the rumor that's going around—that Lieutenant Doran is tangled up in this?"

"You've got a good grapevine. It's true."

"Damn," Cavendish breathed out. "An army officer. That's one to stick in your craw if you're a soldier."

"Yeah, well, just look at it this way—the only reason he *was* army was to carry this plan out."

"Somehow that don't make it any better. You ride with 'em, sleep by them, drink their coffee and their whiskey and then you let them get killed."

Morgan motioned for silence. Even though they expected to be seen, there was no sense in being spotted before they were ready. The Tangles were dead ahead, and that meant Panther. His men held their rifles at the ready now. Glancing back Shell could see that Shirke had achieved the pine-clad bluff.

"They come up out of the Tangles and we ride like hell, Sergeant," Morgan said.

"That's exactly what I had in mind, sir," Cavendish answered.

They entered the badlands slowly, strung out for more than a quarter of a mile. There was no sound to reach Shelter's ears but the whisper of the wind, the creaking of their own saddle leather, and the sound of their horses' hoofs.

There was no sight of Panther, but he was there all right. Walika had said so and Morgan could nearly smell them. The only question was what the renegade's intentions were. Attack all-out, snipe and run, or suck the regiment into a trap?

The last seemed the most likely. If Shirke could be

caught with his pants down in the Tangles he would have no chance at all.

"Keep those weapons at the ready," Morgan said to the young corporal next to him and the word was passed—probably unnecessarily. Every man in that patrol knew what he was riding into.

It had been cool up on the flats with the breeze blowing off the north. Now, in the twisted canyons, it was warm. Morgan could hear the constant hum of insects.

The corporal whose name was Trout had his lip turned back in tense anticipation. Shelter could barely hear him mutter. "They're here, they're here."

Morgan had no doubt about it. The only question was why Panther hadn't hit them yet. Putting himself on the other side of the fence Shelter decided it was this way: Panther had been laying a trap for Shirke's larger force, planning on wiping them out with one concerted attack. Now he had a small exploratory patrol in the Tangles. To strike at the patrol was to alert the rest of the regiment. Yet how far could Panther let them penetrate with the Doran camp not two miles off?

The answer came soon and it came loud. The first burst of gunfire from the bluffs was like a thunderclap; four soldiers were lifted from their saddles to sprawl against the sandy bottom.

"Get the hell out of here!"

The patrol spun, horses bumping into horses as the troopers made a frantic attempt to escape the trap. They made it a hundred feet before Panther closed the door. Rising up from behind dead timber, half a dozen Indian marksmen picked the patrol to pieces. Trout was hit but held on. Cavendish tried to hold a wounded man up by the collar but lost his grip. Shelter ignored his rifle and fired his sixgun into the knot of renegades, having the satisfaction of seeing two of them go down.

"Retreat!" was his command. Retreat to where was another question, since with Panther's men on the bluffs their position was precarious.

The cut in the banks wasn't much protection but it was there that Morgan led his men. Stacked dead timbers formed a natural barricade in front of the half-cave. Shelter hit the ground running. Moving to Trout's horse he helped the young corporal from the saddle and half-carried the wounded man to cover while Cavendish, on one knee, fired wildly at the onrushing Cheyenne.

Cavendish took the belly out of one of the Cheyenne and broke another's knee with his Springfield. Then he too darted for the scant protection the cut provided.

Morgan emptied his Winchester into the band of onrushing renegades. Beside him Trout and Cavendish worked with their slower Springfields. Panther's men fell back, leaving three dead, and the canyon assumed an eerie silence.

"Just the four of us?" Trout asked in a daze.

"Three." Cavendish was hovered over the other trooper. A bullet had clipped the big artery in his thigh and he had died within a minute.

"Holy Christ," Trout muttered.

"How are you?" Shelter asked. Trout had his shirt up, looking at his wound. The bullet had clipped across the front of his belly, leaving flesh hanging in a flap, but he was still lucky. An inch more and his guts would have been spilling out of him.

Trout looked a little paler now that he had seen the wound and touched his own blood. "I'll be all right." He sawed off his shirttail and used it for a bandage. It was soaked through with blood in seconds.

"That'll bring Shirke at the charge anyway," Cavendish said.

"I hope not," Morgan replied. The two men with him waited for an explanation. "It's still the same situation, boys. Panther is up on the bluffs. Shirke rides in to rescue us and he'll get the regiment cut to ribbons."

"Yeah," Trout said softly, reflecting on where that left the three of them—hung out to dry.

A little sand sifted down from above and Morgan drew back quickly, yanking Cavendish. Rifle fire from above peppered the little alcove, with bullets ricocheting in all directions, rock fragments spraying their flesh.

"Anybody hit . . ."

"Here they come again!" Trout shouted and Shelter turned to open up at the fresh charge the renegades had mounted.

Shelter took an Indian through the shoulder, saw him reel and assumed he had gone down as he switched his sights, but the renegade was tough and he made it to the mouth of the niche. Shelter saw him at the last second as he appeared from out of the heavy gunsmoke, hurling himself toward Morgan, hatchet in hand, his mouth open in a bloody war cry.

Shelter ripped upward with the muzzle of his rifle, tearing the throat from the Cheyenne as the hatchet sliced air half an inch from Morgan's skull.

Shell rolled the body aside, got to a knee, and continued to burn ammunition. The renegades eventually pulled back, still firing. Then the silence settled again. Morgan rolled the Indian's body from the cave and reloaded the smoking rifle.

"We can't keep this up for long," Cavendish said.

"How's the ammunition?"

"My pack's on my horse," the sergeant answered grimly. "I got a dozen rounds maybe."

"Trout?"

"The same."

Morgan muttered a curse, levered a fresh round into the breech of his repeater, and sat staring out through the drifting smoke toward the badlands beyond.

"It looks like we're going to have to try getting out of here," he said at last.

"That's the same as suicide, Colonel."

"So's sitting here," Shelter answered.

"Captain Shirke . . ."

"Damn it, he's not going to come riding in here! If he does I'll kick his tail myself."

"Assuming you're alive to do it," Cavendish said grimly. He was looking up toward the rim of the bluff. "Wonder how many of them are up there."

"What's the difference?" Trout asked sourly. "What're we going to do, fly up there? Climb? Shit, a man wouldn't make it six feet."

"Colonel?"

"See any sign of our horses?" Morgan asked.

"Just the dead one."

Shelter smiled thinly. "Then it's got to be up if we go. There's no way we're going to make it through the canyon."

Trout shuddered a little. Morgan didn't blame him at all. The situation was just about hopeless. Their choice came down to sitting where they were, and getting picked off or overwhelmed by a fresh charge, or climbing. Both of those paths seemed to lead to the same place.

"If you've got a plan, then, sir, I'd sure be glad to hear

196

it," Cavendish said, turning his head to spit. Morgan wondered that he could—his own mouth was bone-dry.

"I've got an idea," Shelter said. Not a *plan*. A plan has to assume some hope of success. Just then Morgan had no confidence in anything he could come up with. Hell, they were pinned down, face it, without enough ammunition and with no help coming. All they could do was try *something*.

Morgan told them exactly what he had in mind. When he was finished Trout just stared at him.

"It can't work, sir."

"Got another idea? I'll damn sure take suggestions at this point."

"No, sir," Trout managed a sickly grin. "I got no other ideas. Might as well try it, I guess. Might as well go to hell in a flaming handcart as in a fringed surrey."

Yeah. And hell was about the only place they had a chance of going.

What the hell, Morgan figured, you can only die once.

197

17.

The lull had gone on for too long. The renegades would be streaming across that canyon floor again, but there was no tellling when. It was time to move if they were going to have a chance of living out the day.

Morgan glanced at Cavendish who nodded, wiping a bead of sweat from his eyebrow. Trout also nodded. Whether from a loss of blood or natural fear he was as white as a new-laundered sheet. Shelter wondered what he looked like just then himself. He could feel his dry throat, the set of his jaw. His eyes felt hard and too large for his skull and his heart was moving along at a steady canter.

"Okay," Morgan said finally. There was no point in delaying it any longer. He leaped to his feet and came out of the cave, turning his gun toward the bluff. He saw two heads and one rifle muzzle. The Winchester spewed flame and death. One of the heads was separated from a renegade's body as the other flung himself backward to escape the twisting .44s from Morgan's repeater.

Trout and Cavendish had raced toward the dead white tree and were hoisting it now, tilting it against the face of the bluff as rifle fire from across the canyon began to

198

riddle the bluff face with bullets. Morgan kept his attention on the rim above them. He wasn't going to hit anyone on the far side of the canyon even if he could see them.

Trout was already scrambling up the dead tree, using the broken branches as rungs. Another renegade appeared above and Morgan shot him through the chest. He fell from the rim, passing within a foot of Trout, who was nearly to the top.

Cavendish was right behind him. A shot from across the canyon clipped wood from the dead tree inches from Cavendish's hand. Above, Trout had rolled onto the rim. Morgan saw the renegade dive toward the trooper, but he was in no position to do anything to help Trout.

With the bullets clipping at his heels Shelter started his own mad climb up the tree. He ripped his right hand open and nearly dropped the repeater, but he was suddenly up and over, flat on his belly.

Trout lay beneath a dead Indian. Cavendish must have gotten him. His revolver curled smoke. Shell couldn't give that his attention just now.

Across the canyon a dozen renegades had burst from the brush and their yipping and hollering filled the air along with the popping of their rifles. Their intent was clear: rush across the canyon and follow the escaping whites up the tree. Morgan couldn't see what was going on behind him, but he heard a groan and a scuffling sound.

He was intent on trying to kick the tree away from the bluff and answering the Indian's fire at once. The dead tree slid away in a shower of sand and Shell was able to go to a prone position and tag two more warriors while their bullets whipped past his head.

Cavendish bellied up beside Shelter and began to join the sniping.

"Trout?" Morgan said.

"No," Cavendish said, firing at a running target, hitting it. "Opened up with a knife."

Shelter clamped his jaw and got back to the work at hand. For the moment they had the Indians backing off again, but if they wanted it bad enough, he had no doubt they had the numbers to storm that bluff—or to come around with a circling maneuver.

"We're going to have to get the hell out of here!" Morgan shouted above the report of Cavendish's Springfield.

"And you know where we're going, right?"

"No goddamned idea," Shelter said with a crooked grin.

They were on another of those small mesas that had been produced by years of rain and running water in the Tangles. Each of them was more or less isolated. They were of varying sizes, some miles across, some like this one obviously much smaller. Did Panther have the little mesa surrounded? No telling. But he would, given enough time.

"Now?" Cavendish asked and Shelter nodded. Easing back from the rim the two men started jogging through the sage and scrub oak toward the north, not knowing who they were going to run into or when. It was a gamble—hell, they'd been gambling all day.

A quarter of a mile on Cavendish pulled up, holding his side. A cavalry soldier doesn't do a hell of a lot of running. "You all right, Sergeant?"

"Yeah . . . right . . . give me a minute."

Shelter turned to scan their backtrail. He saw no one

yet, but they would be coming. "We don't have long."

"I know, Colonel, okay." He took a deep breath. "Let's keep going."

The mesa was wider than Shelter thought. It was another fifteen minutes before they reached the north rim, eased up, and had a look over. Nothing was visible. Maybe they had a chance after all.

"You know where we are?" Cavandish asked.

"Yeah, I think I do." He should. They weren't half a mile from the Doran ranch. Morgan would have given a lot to get his hands on that little bastard's throat—and on the sleek white throat of Donna. "How about an offensive mission, Cavendish?"

Cavendish turned and stared, his dirt-streaked face a mask of disbelief. "I know you're kidding me, sir. Attack Panther?"

"No, not Panther. We've squeaked out, it seems. Let Captain Shirke take care of him. How about you and me attacking Doran's crew?"

Cavendish looked at the tall man, unsure if he was joking. When he realized that Shelter was dead serious he whistled. "Where in hell did they ever come up with an officer like you, Morgan? I seen men go battle-crazy, seen officers take a chance for a promotion, some tin medal to wear . . . you're none of those. You're just plain damn mad."

"Yeah. Aren't you?" Shelter asked. Cavendish thought it over for a time, recalling Doran's treachery, the dead bodies he had stacked.

"I guess I am, sir."

On the surface it seemed crazy to return to the ranch, but where else were they going to go? The Indians were behind them and would track them given time. Hell, it was war, why not strike first when it was certain the enemy was going to attack at any time? What had Trout said? "You may as well go to hell in a flaming handcart."

"You've got an idea how we're going to do this, I take it?" Cavendish said.

"Sure." Morgan winked. "Overpower them, Sergeant. Just overpower them."

"Me and my five rounds of ammunition," Cavendish said under his breath. He couldn't decide if Morgan was a hero or a true madman. Yet he had to admit there wasn't much point in hiding in the brush until the renegades found them and took their hair. "Whatever you say, sir, whatever you say."

Morgan clapped him on the shoulder, grinned, and started down the bluff, sliding to the sandy floor of the twisted canyon. He peered into the white sun as Cavendish followed him, wondering if Panther hadn't been watching, waiting, but nothing moved along the canyon floor but a lone droning dragonfly.

Cavendish hit the ground hard and Shelter helped him to his feet. "Which way?"

"North. There's a small feeder canyon ahead and we can follow it right up behind the Doran house."

"They'll have sentries out."

"I doubt it now. They're too busy trying to pull out, I'd guess."

"To join up with Panther?"

"Or make a run for it. Doran didn't strike me as particularly brave. You think he'd stand and fight?"

"If he's sure of winning," Cavendish said.

They jogged up the sandy feeder canyon and then climbed the ridge behind the house. Creeping up the last fifty feet Shelter looked down with satisfaction.

"Still there, anyway." But there was a lot of activity. Around the bunkhouses men were standing with packs and bedrolls. Over at the scorched big house there seemed to be some sort of meeting going on. Shelter couldn't make out any of the figures.

"There's forty men there easy," Cavendish whispered. "Still say we should attack, sir?"

"If we don't they'll be gone in a few minutes. Sure looks like they're trying to run to me."

The sound of a soft footstep behind Shelter caused him to roll and bring his rifle up. He held his fire. Walika stood there grinning, hands up.

"Come looking for you," the Delaware scout said. "Didn't think I'd find you here."

Walika bellied up beside them. Morgan asked, "What's the situation back there?"

"Captain's taking his time. After we heard the fire-fight he redeployed. Trying to flank Panther. You two all that made it out back there?"

Morgan nodded. "I think Shirke's got a chance if he sticks to high ground; tell him that, Walika."

"Sure." The Indian was studying the camp below. "That Doran's gang?"

"It is. If you can get back to Shirke, have him break off a company and send them up here. Best if they can come in from two sides. Say south and east—no one's going to run far the other way, deeper into the Tangles."

"All right," Walika answered. "What're you two going to do?"

"Hold 'em," Shelter said.

"Yeah?" Walika gave a little doubtful shrug. "Good luck." He slapped Cavendish on the shoulder. "I'm gone."

Walika slipped back down the hill and was into the canyon, jogging when the first shots of the battle to the south drifted to Morgan's ears.

"Shirke's hit him," Cavendish said.

"Sounds like you wish you were there."

"Well, sir, I'd rather be there than here," Cavendish answered after sober reflection. "I understand that kind of fighting, anyway. What do we do first?"

"The horses," Shelter said. "This bunch won't be much afoot. With Panther it might be another story, but I'm thinking that if we leave these boys without mounts they won't give us much trouble."

Cavendish was dubious. He lifted his eyes to the ranch again. It was true that most of the horses were still bunched in the corral, but that was on the far side of the ranch, and getting to them was no small problem in itself—let alone what would happen when the white renegades figured out someone was trying to drive them off.

"If you say so," Cavendish said, shaking his head as he started to rise.

Morgan put a hand on his arm. "You're staying here, Sergeant. If I need covering fire you're all I've got." He gave Cavendish his Winchester. The repeater was a hell of a lot faster then the army-issue Springfield.

"We could wait for the company," Cavendish said. Behind them the distant battle continued.

"We could wait, but there's no guarantee Walika will get through, no guarantee that Shirke will be able to cut loose that many men. We don't have much time, Sergeant. These men are getting ready to run. I won't have it." His face grew tense and his voice dropped to a lower pitch. "I won't let the bastards get away now."

Shelter touched Cavendish's shoulder and started on down, circling behind the ridge until he was into the narrow gulley that ran from above the camp to the feeder canyon beyond it. Jogging easily, revolver in hand, Morgan moved through the brushy bottom, his head ducked just slightly. The bluff was six or seven feet high in most places and offered concealment enough.

He came upon the sentry in the last place he had expected it.

The man was squatting behind a bush, his trousers dropped, when Shelter rounded a bend in the gulley. The renegade forgot what he was doing and dove for his rifle.

Shelter was right behind him. Clubbing down at the renegade with the muzzle of his pistol he stung the rifle from the man's hands. Morgan's own Colt went flying, and rolling onto his back as he hit the ground he yanked his bowie from its sheath.

The outlaw was above him now, his own knife in his hand. At least he hadn't yelled out—Morgan meant to see that he didn't have the chance to.

The renegade moved in, ready to hack down with his knife, but Morgan's hand flashed in an underhand movement and the bowie darted upward, burying itself to the hilt in the renegade's throat.

Now the man did try to yell out, but it was to late. Pawing at the knife his cry emerged as a blood-strangled croak. His eyes were wide with pain and disbelief. The knife dropped slowly from his bloody hand as Shelter came to his feet, clapping his hand over the outlaw's mouth, going with him to the ground to hold him there until the death throes stopped.

It took both hands to pull the bowie free. Shelter rolled the body into the brush, recovered his own Colt, and blew the sand from it. Then he started on, cursing the loss of time, but not regretting the taking of a life. That man, whoever he had been, had come here to kill, to be paid for it. He had just run into a little bad luck.

Shelter Morgan.

Morgan was near the head of the gulley. Running in a crouch now he tried to look up and get his bearings. From somewhere he heard voices and he slowed, pressing himself against the bank, waiting until they had faded.

Still distantly he could hear gunfire, much gunfire, and he could only hope Shrike was at least holding his own. He had no real expectation that Shirke would be able to break off a company and send it to the ranch in time to help out. All he had for support was Cavendish on the ridge.

And the enemy was time.

Doran wanted out of there. Fast.

Morgan moved on very slowly now, looking up through the sage that screened the gulley. He could smell a dead fire now—the barn—and he smiled faintly. That, at least, had been a decent attack on the renegades. Maybe, too, it was enough to turn today's battle in Shirke's favor. Morgan knew that Panther's raiders weren't half as well equipped as they would have been had Doran gotten those weapons and ammunition through.

That was past, though. What mattered was the job at hand.

On his belly, Morgan inched up onto the flats, looking toward the corral, dead ahead of him and fifty feet off. He saw two men leading mounts from it and another perched on the corral rails, rifle in his hand, smoke dangling from his lips.

Shelter glanced back toward the big house, wishing

that he could get his hands on Doran, but that was out of the question for now. Then, sucking in his breath, he made his move.

There wasn't time to formulate a plan, and there was no plan that could ensure success. You tried it, and if you lost you lost. Feeling a cold spot in the middle of his spine, Shelter got to his feet and walked out of the gulley, half-expecting a bullet to rip through his back at any moment.

The guard who had his boots hooked on the second rail took a long time before he glanced from his perch at Shelter. When he did his expression didn't even change—on the first look.

The second time he looked, the cigarette fell from his lips and he started to bring the Winchester he carried around. By then Morgan had broken into a run. The snap shot the sentry fired whipped past Shell's head, and Morgan's answering blast from the Colt lifted the outlaw from the rail to fall sprawled against the packed earth of the corral.

The horses began to mill excitedly. Behind Morgan there was a shout, and as Shelter spun he saw a man with a double-ten scattergun taking aim. He flung himself to one side, but the shotgun was never touched off. The hard slap of a distant rifle shot echoed across the valley and the renegade slumped to the ground.

All right, Cavendish, Morgan thought. You can shoot.

He wasn't the only one shooting. Suddenly the air was filled with lead. The horses reared up or panicked and started running for the gate. Morgan helped them along, flagging them out. For the time being he was relatively safe from outlaw lead, but that wouldn't last long.

The big buckskin brushed against him and Shelter

207

caught its mane. Indian style he clung to the side of the horse as they stampeded from the corral.

A renegade appeared in front of Shell, a wild-eyed man with a torn shirt and a sixgun in his meaty hand. Morgan let the buckskin slam him to the ground with its shoulder.

Just for a moment from the heart of the stampeding herd Shelter caught a glimpse of Doran himself running toward the corral, but there was no chance to get a shot off at the blond man. Morgan held his stolen buckskin with the herd and charged through the camp. The renegades, firing their rifles into the air, were trying to halt or turn the herd, but they did more to frighten them on into an even faster run than anything else.

They were abruptly clear of the camp, running through the brush along the feeder canyon. With the herd spread out Morgan went to the back of his buckskin—and immediately brought rifle fire down on himself.

All of the outlaws hadn't been caught flat-footed. There were three mounted men behind him, guns blazing.

Morgan bailed out.

He hit the ground hard, turning an ankle, and dove for the manzanita and sagebrush beside the canyon trail. Bullets tore at the brush, ripping branches from it, plowing into the earth behind Morgan who sat, legs in front of him, two-handing the Colt.

One of the outlaws twisted in the saddle and bounced to the ground to lie still while the others charged on. Morgan's next shot caught one of the horses, a big roan, in the chest and it folded up, rolling head over heels, throwing its rider.

The next squeeze of the trigger did nothing at all. The

hammer fell on an empty chamber, and before Morgan could grab a reload the third outlaw was on top of him.

The bullet from the bluff nearly lifted the top of the renegade's head off. He straightened up suddenly like a man jerked back by unseen wires and then flopped onto his back to lie twitching, already dead.

Cavendish came sliding down the bluff in a shower of dust and stone, lifting Morgan to his feet as Shelter shoveled fresh rounds into the Colt's cylinder.

"They left us two saddled horses," Cavendish said. "I think it's time to use them, sir."

The man was right. Up the canyon another half-dozen riders came, their horses' hoofs pounding against the earth. Shell was aboard the blaze-faced sorrel and out of there, Cavendish on his tail.

They wound through the maze of canyons for another mile and then climbed to high ground again. The searchers came driving up the canyon in a hell of a lather, but Morgan and Cavendish let them go on by—there was no sense in tempting fate one more time when it wasn't necessary. By the time that little band of renegades figured out that they had lost their quarry, they would also have had time to reflect that it was high time to get shut of Dakota and Doran's grand schemes of empire.

To the south they could still hear gunfire. Now, Cavendish, hands on hips, his uniform soaked through with perspiration, pointed out dust moving their way.

"Looks like Shirke managed to break off a company after all."

And that meant that he had Panther on the run or contained—he wasn't going to short the regiment to go on to a secondary target if possible.

"And now?" Cavendish asked, squatting with the horse's reins, allowing himself a grin of relief.

"Now," Shelter Morgan said, "we finish it."

Cavendish, who had seen enough of this madman's work, asked cautiously, "We're waiting for the company, aren't we, sir?"

Shell now grinned. "Yeah. We're waiting for the company. I'm only half a madman. When they have the valley flanked, we're going back down."

"And find Doran?"

"And find Doran. And put him out of his misery."

18.

It was two in the afternoon when the company of soldiers put in their appearance. Cavendish knew their leader and he stood, waving a hand.

"Bellows, hey, Bellows!"

Bellows, a grizzled sergeant with blood on his tunic, swung that way and saluted, "Yes, sir, Lieutenant Cavendish," and then saluted Shell, "Howdy, Colonel."

Cavendish, who had forgotten completely that he was supposed to be an acting lieutenant and had been ready to ask Bellows who his officer was, paused and then grinned sheepishly. "Me, huh? I'm it?"

"You or the colonel, however it stands. Michaelson has B Company and they're still trading lead with Panther."

"We going to win that one?" Morgan asked.

"Looks like it, sir. They seem real low on ammo now. An Indian's quick with a bow an' arrow, quicker than most of us with a rifle, but you don't carry so many charges, do you? No, once they started to seem shy about answering our fire Shirke closed the clamps on 'em real quick. Most of Panther's people are caught in a blind canyon back there—some of 'em took to their heels.

211

What's the situation here?"

"Let's have a look," Morgan suggested.

"Corporal Gentry's got the column coming in from the north," Bellows told the others as they rode. "It'll take him a little longer being as he's got to circle, but he'll close it off good. I told him my signal was three shots—assuming we don't draw a lot of fire before we have a chance to do any signaling."

"All right, good." Morgan twisted in his saddle. It was reassuring to see men riding behind him who were actually on his side.

"How many they got?" Bellows asked.

"Forty some," Morgan answered. "Most of them will be foot soldiers now."

"Will they?" Bellows liked that, he liked it very much.

"They'll do one of two things," Shelter said. "Hole up—in which case they'll be our meat for the taking—or make a run. If they try to run, they'll have to try to go north and that'll bring them up against Corporal Gentry and his patrol. I hope Gentry isn't shy about shooting civilians."

"Not this kind," Cavendish said, taking a swallow from Bellow's canteen. "Don't worry about that. Gentry had family settling in the Trace. He knows what to do."

There was still a lot of daylight left when they crested the ridge and looked down at the Doran ranch for the last time. Morgan sat his captured horse and studied it closely.

"They there, sir?" Bellows asked.

"I'll wager some of them are. What do you think, Cavendish?"

"I know how to find out," the NCO said.

"You want to send a squad in to have a look?"

"If it's all right with you, sir—unless you'd rather do it alone," he added with a smile.

"Enough is enough for anybody, Lieutenant Cavendish. Take charge. First sign of activity, get the hell out of there and take cover. We'll get them out of there if we have to starve them out—there's no hurry now, none at all. I just want to make sure we get all of them."

Cavendish nodded. *Doran.* The colonel meant Doran. Yeah, he wanted the son of a bitch too. He chose four men to go down with him while the other cavalry soldiers took up positions along the ridge. Shelter looked northward, seeing no sign yet of the second contingent. Still to the south there was sporadic firing, but it was mop-up time down there now. Shirke had come through for them in the end.

Cavendish and his people advanced on foot. A horse meant a quicker getaway in case of trouble, but a gunshot-panicked horse could be more of a liability than an asset.

They didn't make it far before gunfire erupted from within the big house and the bunkhouse across the way. Cavendish's picket line broke to a ragged retreat. Two men went down and another was limping. Cavendish himself dove behind a trough and lay there, pinned down.

Bellows said in a slow drawl, "I count maybe six, ten guns, sir. The others must be long gone."

Morgan nodded. He had seen a target. A silhouette behind a curtained upstairs window had caught his eye and he sighted on it as Gentry spoke. He squeezed off evenly and saw his bullet smash through the glass. A second later a man tumbled through it to the ground below, his rifle falling free.

"Like I said, maybe five, nine guns," Bellows said.

213

"What do you want to do, sir?"

"Give them a chance to surrender."

"*Them?*"

"One chance. Take it or leave it."

For some reason a man chose to run. They saw him burst from the back door and try racing toward the gulley. He didn't make it far. The guns of Cavendish's men chopped him down and left him lying on the hard earth.

"How about a little show of force?" Bellows suggested and Morgan nodded. The entire patrol lined up along the ridge and began firing in unison. Bullets sang off the stonework of the lower story and riddled the wood and glass upstairs.

"All right, hold your fire," Morgan said and Bellows lifted his hand in signal. Shelter took three steps forward, cupped his hands to his mouth, and called out to the scorched and bullet-pocked house below.

"This is your only chance! Come out of there now or we'll cut you down. No one's going to run, no one's going to stand off the army. Make your choice. You've got a minute!"

It took them less than half of that to give it up and emerge from the buildings with their hands raised. Some of them might hang for what they had done, but they must have figured they had a chance as long as they were alive. They had none if they stayed there to try shooting it out with the army.

Morgan rode down at the head of the column. The prisoners had been herded up into a small knot and were searched.

"Where's Doran?" he asked a bearded warrior.

The man spat. "Took off at the first sign of trouble.

Told us to wait for him here and hold the fort."

"North?" Morgan asked, lifting his eyes.

"Yeah, I think so."

"They're yours, Cavendish," Morgan said, nodding at the prisoners.

"If you don't mind, sir, I'd like to go with you."

Morgan studied the man's face for a minute and then nodded. "All right. Bellows, you're in charge then. I'll take half of your people. Count 'em out for me."

"Every other man!" Bellows shouted. Morgan was already back in the saddle, and with Cavendish beside him he led the patrol out northward.

That was where the dog had run.

"Got him," Cavendish said quietly. "He'll meet Gentry's patrol sure as hell."

He had no more than gotten the words out when they heard the distant firing. To the north. Yeah, Doran had run into something he hadn't expected.

"Let's have it at a gallop, Cavendish," Morgan said, lifting his own horse from its walk. It was time. Shelter didn't want to miss out on seeing when Doran went down to lie in the sand in a pool of his own blood.

Before they had crested the next hill they could see smoke rising above the pines, and when they cleared the trees they saw the desperate men pinned down in a narrow grassless valley. Gentry had done his job properly. He had Doran's raiders pinned down on open ground with his own column divided on either side of them. It was plain murderous. Men lay behind their dead horses firing back at the army patrol. They must have known it was futile, but the renegade whites continued to fight like rabid dogs.

"Here's some gravy for us," Cavendish said with

215

unconcealed pleasure.

He was right. Ten or twelve raiders had broken free of the trap and were riding like hell directly toward Shelter's patrol. They never had a chance.

One of the renegades spotted a blue uniform and shouted out. The raiders opened fire and the army rifles barked a response. They tried to turn, but that ran them right back toward Gentry's guns.

Except for one man who swung to the east, toward the Tangles.

Doran.

"Let's get him!" Cavendish, who had also seen the blond rider, shouted with sheer exhilaration. Morgan's hand fell on the NCO's wrist.

"Uh-uh. No. He's my meat, Sergeant, all the way."

"Sir . . ." Whatever else Cavendish had to say was cut off by Shelter's sharp order.

"Close the noose on those in the valley, Cavendish. Mount your charge." Then Shell heeled his horse, heeled it hard and lifted it into a dead run. Doran was dead ahead of him, his horse faltering. Grim satisfaction flooded through Shelter.

It was time to pay.

To pay for the dead and intimidated and orphaned and crippled Doran had caused with his ambitious scheme to grab the land beyond Little Trace for himself and his army of thugs.

Shelter shouldered his Winchester, but from the back of a running horse he didn't have much chance. The bullet whipped by Doran close enough to cause him to turn and look back over his shoulder at the tall man pursuing him. His face went ashen, his eyes opened wide. Morgan punched another round through the Winchester

216

and watched with gratification as Doran slapped at his shoulder and slumped in the saddle.

There wasn't much time. Morgan's horse was fresher and he was closing the gap between himself and Doran, but the badlands stood dead ahead, wild, tangled, and all-concealing.

Doran's palomino dipped into a ravine and came up the other side—riderless. Shelter threw himself from his saddle as a bullet hummed past his ear and sent his horse rearing.

He had Doran then. Or did Doran have him?

The two of them alone in the brushy bottom of one of the Tangles' thousand canyons. There was distant gunfire, but it sounded no louder than the humming of the cicadas in the canyon just then. Morgan's horse took a hobbled step and it lifted its head, looking into the brush beyond. Sage, cholla, manzanita, and dry cattails clotted the bottom here. It was almost impossible to move without rattling dried brush.

Morgan didn't move. He was on his belly, the sand beneath him warm, the air moving through the brush cold. The big Colt was in his hand, deadly and reassuring.

A cottontail bounded away and Shelter's eyes shifted that way. He couldn't see a thing, couldn't hear anything but the wind.

Then the man was there. Bursting from the brush with a gun in hand, his shoulder streaming blood, Doran was there and he drilled the sand around Morgan's body with his .44 revolver.

Shelter was slower, but his aim was more accurate. The first bullet he sent Doran's way tagged the bad shoulder again, half turning him. The second caught him low on the back as he spun away.

217

Morgan got to his feet and walked toward the renegade, who still managed to keep his feet somehow.

He turned to Shelter, bringing his gun up for the last time. "Can't kill me," Doran said. His voice was wooden, half-astonished, half-challenging. He was trying to pull the trigger of his pistol which suddenly seemed too heavy for him to aim steadily.

"The hell I can't," Shelter Morgan said and he sent a third bullet into the tortured body of the renegade, this one stopping the twisted brain that had caused so many other deaths.

Shelter stood over the body of the army officer until the cicadas recovered from the explosive sounds of gunshots and started chirping again and Cavendish on a big army bay rode up on the sandy bank behind Morgan to look down at the scene. Then he turned, holstered his Colt, and said to Cavendish, "Let's go home. It's over."

19.

There wasn't much to wrap-up at Shirke's Fort Randall office. Panther had bought it—no one knew who had shot him, but there were several dozen people who wanted to take credit for it. Doran was dead, saving the army the embarrassment of a court-martial and execution. A few of the renegades, white and red, had made their escape, but they weren't likely to be back to cause trouble. Lieutenant Ball had taken a bullet in the leg—trying to drag an enlisted man from trouble—but Dr. Finney said it wasn't all that serious. Star Dan had astonished everyone by opening his eyes one day and saying, "Doc, my head hurts, but I think I want to get up and move around a bit," and then doing it.

Shirke briefed Morgan, Michaelson, and Cavendish on his final copy of the report and asked if Shelter had anything to add.

"Very little. Just strike my name," Morgan told the captain. "General Pomfret and I are kind of shy about publicity. A few other things." He nodded at Cavendish. "That temporary second-lieutenant's bar ought to stay on this man's epaulet. A promotion for Corporal Gentry would be in order. And Bellows ought to at least get a citation. Another stripe along with that would be fitting."

Morgan rose and Shirke looked at him with those watery eyes of his, "Surely you're not leaving now, Colonel? I had a special dinner planned."

"I'm leaving." He had a few plans of his own, centered around the little red-headed girl at the hotel in Rosalia.

"If anything should come of this . . ."

"Handle it yourself, Captain. I was never here. General Pomfret doesn't know anything about it. Luck to all of you . . . By the way, tell Ball that he's on my list— as a man who's on his way back to being a good officer."

Shirke started to rise, to salute, but the tall man was already out the door. A new first sergeant was at the desk in the orderly room. Stoner, deservedly, was sitting in the stockade waiting for his court-martial for misappropriation and the attempted murder of Star Dan, who it seemed was able to testify now.

Morgan had an army bay to ride now and he aimed toward the main gate of Fort Randall. The stars were bright in a cold sky, and ahead a warm-blooded woman waiting for him.

She was there and when Morgan toed open the hotel-room door she was naked from the waist up, reclining under a white satin sheet that the hotel sure hadn't provided.

"You make a woman wait too long, big man," Boomer Kennedy said, patting the mattress beside her.

"Sorry. Got hung up," Shelter said. His shirt was already off and now he kicked off his boots and dropped his trousers, moving to Boomer who eyed his erection with hunger, reaching for it with both hands.

"Hell, I guess it was worth waiting for," she said,

dragging him down to her as she flipped the sheet aside, displaying her lush, eager young body, all curves and declivities, ripe breasts with swollen pink nipples, and downy patch of reddish hair nestled between her smooth white thighs.

Morgan's mouth met hers and his hand slipped between those thighs finding a warm, damp haven. He was rolling nearer to her when the hotel door thudded open and the crazy woman burst in.

Her hair was tangled, her eyes red and wild, her skirt and blouse torn open, and as Morgan turned sharply, Donna Drake lifted her Rimington revolver and sighted it at him.

"You dirty, dirty bastard!" she panted.

The roar of the gun filled the room with sudden death and powder smoke, but it hadn't come from the Remington. Boomer Kennedy had her big old rifle in her hands and the muzzle curled smoke. Donna Drake lay on the floor, blood smearing her lovely breasts.

"Damn all, Morgan," Boomer whispered, lowering her rifle.

"What were you doing with that thing in bed?" Shelter asked.

"You . . . well, hell, Morgan, you know I been telling you you just don't know how to take care of yourself."

"How about you?" Shell asked, drawing the naked woman to him. "Do I know how to take care of you?"

There were running footsteps in the hall, people rushing toward their door. Boomer kissed Morgan and said, "Damn right you take good care of me. Let's find us a new room and you can prove it again."

She started toward the door, naked, rifle still in hand, Shell's arm around her. "Wait a minute," she said.

Returning to the bed she snatched the satin sheets from it. "Six bucks for these, and when we do it, it's going to be done right. I've been waiting forever for you to come back, big man."

Boomer wrapped the sheets around her and together they went out into the hall and past the gawkers and the curiosity-seekers. Shelter owed her one again.

And she was going to get it.

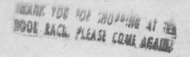

THE SURVIVALIST SERIES
by Jerry Ahern

ACTION ADVENTURE

SILENT WARRIORS (1675, $3.95)
by Richard P. Henrick
The Red Star, Russia's newest, most technologically advanced submarine, outclasses anything in the U.S. fleet. But when the captain opens his sealed orders 24 hours early, he's staggered to read that he's to spearhead a massive nuclear first strike against the Americans!

THE PHOENIX ODYSSEY (1789, $3.95)
by Richard P. Henrick
All communications to the USS *Phoenix* suddenly and mysteriously vanish. Even the urgent message from the president cancelling the War Alert is not received. In six short hours the *Phoenix* will unleash its nuclear arsenal against the Russian mainland.

COUNTERFORCE (2013, $3.95)
Richard P. Henrick
In the silent deep, the chase is on to save a world from destruction. A single Russian Sub moves on a silent and sinister course for American shores. The men aboard the U.S.S. *Triton* must search for and destroy the Soviet killer Sub as an unsuspecting world races for the apocalypse.

EAGLE DOWN (1644, $3.75)
by William Mason
To western eyes, the Russian Bear appears to be in hibernation—but half a world away, a plot is unfolding that will unleash its awesome, deadly power. When the Russian Bear rises up, God help the Eagle.

DAGGER (1399, $3.50)
by William Mason
The President needs his help, but the CIA wants him dead. And for Dagger—war hero, survival expert, ladies man and mercenary extraordinaire—it will be a game played for keeps.

Available wherever paperbacks are sold, or order direct from the Publisher. Send cover price plus 50¢ per copy for mailing and handling to Zebra Books, Dept. 2148, 475 Park Avenue South New York, N.Y. 10016. Residents of New York, New Jersey and Pennsylvania must include sales tax. DO NOT SEND CASH.